A MAN

and

A WOMAN

STANLEY WATERLOO

1st WORLD
LIBRARY
Literary Society

A Man and a Woman

Stanley Waterloo

© 1st World Library, 2006
PO Box 2211
Fairfield, IA 52556
www.1stworldlibrary.com
First Edition

LCCN: 2006938106

Softcover ISBN: 978-1-4218-3406-1
Hardcover ISBN: 978-1-4218-3306-4
eBook ISBN: 978-1-4218-3506-8

Purchase *"A Man and a Woman"*
as a traditional bound book at:
www.1stWorldLibrary.com/purchase.asp?ISBN=978-1-4218-3406-1

1st World Library is a literary, educational organization
dedicated to:

- Creating a free internet library of downloadable ebooks

- Hosting writing competitions and offering book
publishing scholarships.

Interested in more 1st World Library books?
contact: literacy@1stworldlibrary.com
Check us out at: www.1stworldlibrary.com

1st World Library Literary Society

Giving Back to the World

"If you want to work on the core problem, it's early school literacy."

- James Barksdale, former CEO of Netscape

"No skill is more crucial to the future of a child, or to a democratic and prosperous society, than literacy."

- Los Angeles Times

Literacy... means far more than learning how to read and write... The aim is to transmit... knowledge and promote social participation."

- UNESCO

"Literacy is not a luxury, it is a right and a responsibility. If our world is to meet the challenges of the twenty-first century we must harness the energy and creativity of all our citizens."

- President Bill Clinton

"Parents should be encouraged to read to their children, and teachers should be equipped with all available techniques for teaching literacy, so the varying needs and capacities of individual kids can be taken into account."

- Hugh Mackay

CONTENTS

CHAPTER I

PROLOGUE

But for a recent occurrence I should certainly not be telling the story of a friend, or, rather, I should say, of two friends of mine. What that occurrence was I will not here indicate—it is unnecessary; but it has not been without its effect upon my life and plans. If it be asked by those who may read these pages under what circumstances it became possible for me to acquire such familiarity with certain scenes and incidents in the lives of one man and one woman,—scenes and incidents which, from their very nature, were such that no third person could figure in them,—I have only to explain that Grant Harlson and I were friends from boyhood, practically from babyhood, and that never, during all our lives together, did a change occur in our relationship. He has told me many things of a nature imparted by one man to another very rarely, and only when each of the two feels that they are very close together in that which sometimes makes two men as one. He was proud and glad when he told me these things—they were but episodes, and often trivial ones—and I was interested deeply. They added the details of a history much of which I knew and part of which I had guessed at.

He was not quite the ordinary man, this Grant Harlson, close friend of mine. He had an individuality, and his name is familiar to many people in the world. He has been looked upon by the tactful as but one of a type in a new nationality—a type with traits not yet clearly defined, a type not large, nor yet, thank God, uncommon—one of the best of the type; to me, the best. A close friend perhaps is blind. No; he is not that: he but sees so clearly that the world, with poorer view, may not always agree with him.

I hardly know how to describe this same Grant Harlson. At this stage of my story it is scarcely requisite that I should, but the account is loose and vagrant and with no chronology. Physically, he was more than most men, six feet in height, deep of chest, broad-shouldered, strong-legged and strong-featured, and ever in good health, so far as all goes, save the temporary tax on recklessness nature so often levies, and the other irregular tax she levies by some swoop of the bacilli of which the doctors talk so much and know so little. I mean only that he might catch a fever with a chill addition if he lay carelessly in some miasmatic swamp on some hunting expedition, or that, in time of cholera, he might have, like other men, to struggle with the enemy. But he tossed off most things lightly, and had that vitality which is of heredity, not built up with a single generation, though sometimes lost in one. Forest and farm-bred, college-bred, city-fostered and broadened and hardened. A man of the world, with experiences, and in his quality, no doubt, the logical, inevitable result of such experiences—one with a conscience flexile and seeking, but hard as rock when once satisfied. One who never, intentionally, injured a human being, save for equity's sake. One who, of course, wandered in looking for what was, to him, the right, but who, having once determined, was ever steadfast. A man who had seen and known and fed and felt and risked, but who seemed to me always as if his religion were: "What shall I do? Nature says so-and-so, and the Power beyond rules nature." Laws of organization for political purposes, begun before Romulus and Remus, and varied by the dale-grouped Angles or the Northmen's Thing, did not seem to much impress him. He recognized their utility, wanted to improve them, made that his work, and eventually observed most of them. This, it seemed to me, was his honest make-up—a Berseker, a bare-sark descendant of the Vikings, in a dress-coat. He had passions, and gratified them sometimes. He had ambitions, and worked for them. He had a conscience, and was guided by it.

It was always interesting to me to look at him in youthful fray, more so, years afterward, in club or in convention, or anywhere, and try to imagine him the country small boy. Keen, hard, alert in all the ways of a great city, it was difficult to conceive him in his early youth, well as I knew it; difficult to reflect that his dreams at night were not of the varying results of some late scheme, nor of white shoulders at the opera, nor the mood of the Ninth Ward, nor of the drift of business, but of some farm-house's front yard in mid-summer with a boy aiming a long shot-gun at a red-winged poacher in a cherry tree, or that he saw, in sleep, the worn jambs beside the old-fashioned fireplace where, winter mornings, he kicked on his frozen boots, and the living-room where, later in the morning, he ate so largely of buckwheat cakes. He was a figure, wicked some said, a schemer many said, a rock of refuge for his friends said more. This was the man, no uncommon type in the great cities of the great republic.

As for the woman, I write with greater hesitation. I can tell of her in this place but in vague outline. She was slender, not tall, brown-haired and with eyes like those of the deer or Jersey heifer, save that they had the accompanying expression of thought or mood or fancy which mobile human features with them give. She was a woman of the city, with all that gentle craft which is a woman's heritage. She was good. She was unlike all others in the world to one man—no, to two.

I have but tried to tell what these two people appeared to me. I can see them as they were, but cannot tell it as I should. I have not succeeded well in expressing myself in words. Even were I cleverer, I should fail. We can picture characters but approximately.

CHAPTER II

CLOSE TO NATURE

The great forest belt, oak, ash, beech and maple, sweeps southwestward from New England through New York and trends westward and even to the north again till one sees the same landscape very nearly reproduced in Wisconsin wilds. Not far from where its continuity is broken by the southern reach of Lake Huron was a clearing cut in the wood. The land was rolling, and through the clearing ran a vigorous creek, already alder-fringed—for the alder follows the chopper swiftly—and glittering with countless minnows. In the spring great pickerel came up, too, from the deep waters, miles away, to spawn and, sometimes, to be speared. From either side of the creek the ground ascended somewhat, and on one bank stood a little house. It was a house pretentious for the time, since it was framed and boarded instead of being made of logs, but it contained only three rooms: one, the general living-room with the brick fireplace on one side, and the others smaller, for sleeping apartments. So close to the edge of the forest was the house that the sweep of the wind through the tree-tops made constant music, and the odd, squalling bark of the black squirrel, the chatter of the red one, the drumming of the ruffed grouse, the pipe of the quail and the morning gobble of the wild turkey were familiar sounds. There were deer and bear in the depths of the green ocean, and an occasional wolverine. Sometimes at night a red fox would circle about the clearing and bark querulously, the cry contrasting oddly with the notes of whippoorwills and the calls of loons. The trees were largely oak and beech and ash and birch, and in the spring there were great splashes of white where the June berry trees had burst into bloom. In summer there was a dense greenness everywhere, and in autumn a great blaze of scarlet and yellow leaves.

There was an outlined flower garden in front of the house, made in virgin soil, and with the stumps of trees, close-hewn, still showing above the surface. Beside the door were what they called "bouncing Betties" and "old hen and chickens," and on each side of a short pathway, that led to what was as yet little more than a trail through the wood, were bunches of larkspur and phlox and old-fashioned pinks and asters, and there were a few tall hollyhocks and sunflowers standing about as sentinels. The wild flowers all about were so close to these that all their perfumes blended, and the phlox and pinks could see their own cousins but a few feet away. The short path ran through a clump of bushes but a few yards from the creek. In these bushes song-sparrows and "chippy-birds" built their nests.

In the doorway of the little house by the forests edge stood, one afternoon in summer, a young man. He was what might perhaps be termed an exceedingly young man, as his sixth birthday was but lately attained, and his stature and general appearance did not contradict his age. His apparel was not, strictly speaking, in keeping with the glory of the general scene. His hat had been originally of the quality known as "chip," but the rim was gone, and what remained had an air of abandon about it. His clothing consisted of two garments, a striped, hickory shirt and trousers of blue drilling. The trousers were supported by suspenders, home-made, of the same material. Sometimes he wore but one. It saved trouble. He was barefooted. He stood with a hand in each pocket, his short legs rather wide apart, and looked out upon the landscape. His air was that of a large landed proprietor, one, for instance, who owned the earth.

This young man under consideration had not been in society to any great extent, and of one world had seen very little. Of another he knew a great deal, for his age. With people of the sort who live in towns he was unacquainted, but with nature's people he was on closer terms. He had a great friend and crony in a person who had been a teacher, and who had come to this frontier life from a broader field. This person was his mother. With his father he was also on a relationship of familiarity, but the father was, necessarily, out with his axe most of the time, and so it came that the young man and his mother were more literally growing up together with the country. To her he went with such problems as his great mind failed to solve, and he had come to have a very good opinion of her indeed. Not that she was as wise as he in many things; certainly not. She did not know how the new woodchuck hole was progressing, nor where the coon tracks were thickest along the creek, nor where the woodpecker was nesting; but she was excessively learned, nevertheless, and could be relied upon in an emergency. He approved of her, decidedly. Besides, he remembered her course on one occasion when he was in a great strait. He was but three years old then, but he remembered all about it. It was, in fact, this occurrence which had given him his hobby.

The young man had a specialty. He had several specialties, but to one yielded all the rest. He had an eye to chipmunks, and had made most inefficient traps for them and hoped some day to catch one, but they were nothing to speak of. As for the minnows in the creek, had he not caught one with a dipper once, and had he not almost hit a big pickerel with a stone? He knew where the liverwort and anemones grew most thickly in the spring and had gathered fragrant bunches of them daily, and he knew, too, of a hollow where there had been a snowy sheet of winter-green blossoms earlier, and where there would soon be an abundance of red berries such as his mother liked. At beech-nut gathering, in the season, he admitted no superior. As for the habits of the yellow-birds, particularly at the season when they were feeding upon thistle-seed and made a golden cloud amid the white one as they drifted with the down, well, he was the only one who really knew anything about it! Who but he could take the odd-shaped pod of the wild fleur-de-lis, the common flag, and, winding it up in the flag's own long, narrow leaf, holding one end, and throwing the pod sling-wise, produce a sound through the air like that of the swoop of the night-hawk? And who better than he could pluck lobelia, and smart weed, and dig wild turnips and bring all for his mother to dry for possible use, should, he or his father or she catch cold or be ill in any way? Hopes for the future had he, too. Sometimes a deer had come in great leaps across the clearing, and once a bear had invaded the hog-pen. The young man had an idea that as soon as he became a little taller and could take down the heavy gun, an old "United States yager" with a big bore, bloodshed would follow in great quantities. He had persuaded his father to let him aim the piece once or twice, and had confidence that if he could get a fair shot at any animal, that animal would die. Were it a deer, he had concluded he would aim from a great stump a few feet distant from the house. If a bear came, he would shut the door and raise the window, not too far, and blaze away from there. But in none of all these things, either present exploits or imaginings for the future, was his interest most entangled. His specialty was Snakes.

Not intended by nature for a naturalist was this youthful individual whose specialty was snakes. Very much enamored was he of most of nature's products, but not at all of the family *ophidia*. Snakes were his specialty simply because he did not approve of them. All dated back to the affair of three years before. Snakes were abundant in the wood, but were not of many kinds. There were garter-snakes, dreaded of the little frogs, but timid of most things; there was a small snake of wonderful swiftness and as green as the grass into which it darted; there were the water pilots, sunning themselves in coils upon the driftwood in the water, swart of color, thick of form and offensive of aspect; there were the milk-snakes, yellowish gray, with wonderful banded sides and with checker-board designs in black upon their yellow bellies. Sometimes a pan of milk from the solitary cow, set for its cream in the dug-out cellar beneath the house, would be found with its yellow surface marred and with a white puddling about the floor, and then the milk remaining would be thrown away and there would be a washing and scalding of the pan, because the thief was known. There were, in the lowlands, the massasaugas; short, sluggish rattle-snakes, venomous but cowardly, and, finally, there were the black-snake ranging everywhere, for no respecter of locality is *bascanion constrictor* when in pursuit of prey. Largest of all the snakes of the region, the only constrictor among them, at home in the lowlands, on the hillsides or in the tree-tops, the black-snake was the dread of all small creatures of the wood. There was a story of how one of them had dropped upon a hunter, coiled himself about his neck and strangled him.

This young man of six remembered how, one day, three years back, before he had assumed trousers or become familiar with all the affairs of the world, he was alone in the house, his mother having gone into the little garden. He remembered how, looking up, he saw, lifted above the doorsill, a head with beady, glittering eyes, and how, after a moment's survey, the head was lifted higher and there came gliding over the floor toward him a black monster, with darting tongue and long, curved body and evident fierce intent. He remembered how he leaped for a high stool which served him at the table, how he clambered to its top and there set up a mighty yell for succor—for he had great lungs. He could, by shutting his eyes, even now, see his mother as she came running from the garden, see her look of terror as she caught sight of the circling thing upon the floor, and then the look of desperation as the mother instinct rose superior and she dashed into the room, seized the great iron shovel that stood before the fireplace, and began dealing reckless blows at the hissing serpent. A big black-snake is not a pleasant customer, but neither—for a black-snake—is a frenzied mother with an iron fire shovel in her hand, and this particular snake turned tail, a great deal of it, by the way, since it extended to its head, and disappeared over the doorsill in a cataract of black and into the wood again.

From that hour the individual so beleaguered on a stool had been no friend of snakes. Talk about vendettas! No Sicilian feud was ever bitterer or more relentlessly pursued, as the boy increased in size and confidence. Scores of garter-snakes had been his victims; once even a milk-snake had yielded up the ghost, and once—a great day that—he had seen a black-snake in the open and had assailed it valorously with stones hurled from a distance. When it came toward him he retreated, but did not abandon the bombardment, and finally drove it into a cover of deep bushes. Come to close quarters with a black-snake he had never done, for a double reason: firstly, because stones did almost as well as a club, and, secondly, because his father, fearing for him, had threatened him with punishment if he essayed such combat, and the firm old rule of "spare the rod and spoil the child" was adhered to literally by the father and indorsed by the mother with hesitation. And, growing close to the house, were slender sprouts of birch and willow, each of which leaned forward as if to say, "I am just the thing to lick a boy with," and such a sprout as one of these, especially the willow, does, under proper conditions, so embrace one's shoulders and curl about one's legs and make itself familiar. But the feud was on, and as a permanency, though, on this particular afternoon, the young man, as he stood there in the doorway, had no thought of snakes. Something else this summer was attracting much of his attention. He had a family on his hands.

CHAPTER III

BOY, BIRD AND SNAKE

The young man's family was not large, but a part of it was young, and he felt the responsibility. The song-sparrow is the very light and gladness of the woods and fields. There are rarer singers, and birds of more brilliant plumage, but he is the constant quantity. His notes may not rival those mellow, brief ones of the blue-birds in early spring, so sweet in their quaint inflection, which suggest all hope, and are so striking because heard while snow may be yet upon the ground; he may not have the wild abandon of the bobolink with that tinkle and gurgle and thrill; he is no pretentious songster, like a score of other birds, but he is a great part of the soul of early summer, for he is telling, morning, noon and night, how good the world is, how he approves of the sunshine, and how everything is all right! And so the young man approved much of the song-sparrow, and was interested in the movements of all his kind.

One day in May, the boy had noted something in the clump of bushes, between the house and creek, which very much resembled a small bird's-nest, and had at once investigated. He found it, the nest of the song-sparrow, and, when the little gray guardian had fluttered away, he noted the four tiny eggs, and their mottled beauty. He did not touch them, for he had been well trained as to what should be the relations between human beings and all singing birds, but his interest in the progress of that essay in summer housekeeping became at once absorbing. He announced in the house that he intended to watch over the nest all summer, and keep off the hawks, and that when the little eggs were hatched, and the little birds were grown, maybe he would try to tame one. He was encouraged in the idea. It is good to teach a boy to be protective. And when the birds were hatched, his interest deepened.

He was half inclined, as he stood in the doorway on this particular day, to visit the dense bushes and note the condition of affairs in that vicinity, but, buoyant as he was, there was something in the outlook which detained him. There was such a yellow glory to the afternoon, and so many things were happening.

Balanced above the phlox, a humming-bird, green-backed and glittering, hung and tasted for a moment, then flashed to where the larkspurs were. A red-headed woodpecker swung downward on the wing to the white-brown side of a dead elm, sounded a brief tattoo upon the surface, then dived at a passing insect. A phoebe bird was singing somewhere. A red squirrel sat perched squarely on the drooping limb of a hickory tree and chewed into a plucked nut, so green that the kernel was not formed, then dropped it to the ground, and announced in a chatter that he was a person of importance. Great yellow butterflies, with black markings upon their wings, floated lazily here and there, and at last settled in a magnificent cluster upon a moist spot in a mucky place where something pleased their fancy, and where they fed and fluttered tremulously. There were myriads of wild bees, and a pleasant droning filled the air, while from all about came the general soft clamor of the forest, made up of many sounds.

The boy was satisfied with the prospect. Suddenly he started. There was a call which was not of peacefulness. He knew the cry. He had heard it when some bird of prey had seized a smaller one. It was the call of the sparrow now, and it came from his clump of bushes. His family was in danger. A hawk, perhaps, but he would have seen such a foe in its descent. It might be a cat-bird or a weasel?

With a rush, the boy was across the garden, and as he ran he snatched up what was for a person of such inches an ideal club, a cut of hickory, perhaps two feet in length, not over an inch in thickness, but tough and heavy enough for a knight errant of his years. He broke through the slight herbage about the place where the bushes grew thickest, and, getting into an open space, had a fair view of the particular shrub wherein were the bird's-nest and his birdlings. He stopped short and looked, then ran back a little, then looked again, and straightway there rose from his throat a scream which, though greater in volume, was almost in its character like that other wild cry of the two sparrows who were fluttering pitifully and desperately about their nest, tempting their own death each instant in defense of their half-fledged young. He stood with his youthful limbs half paralyzed, and screamed, for he saw what was most horrible, and what it seemed he could not check nor hinder, though a cruel tragedy was going on before his eyes!

Curled easily about the main stem of the bush, close to which, upon a forked limb, rested the sparrow's nest, its dark coils reaching downward and its free neck and head waving regularly to and fro, was a monstrous black-snake, and in its jaws fluttered feebly one of the youthful sparrows. Evidently the seizure had just been made when the boy burst in upon the scene. The snake's eyes glittered wickedly, and it showed no disposition to drop its prey because of the intruder. It only reared its head and swung slowly from side to side. Lying almost at full length upon a branching limb of the same bush, and on a level with the nest, was a second serpent, its head raised slightly, but motionless, awaiting, it seemed, its opportunity to seize another of the tender brood. The parent birds flew about in converging circles in their strait, clamoring piteously and approaching dangerously near to the jaws of their repulsive enemies. The boy but stood and screamed. They were the greatest black-snakes he had ever seen. Then, all at once, he became another creature. His childish voice changed in its key, and, club in hand, screaming still louder, he ran right at the bush. At the same moment his frightened mother came running down the pathway, screaming also.

As the boy leaped downward, both snakes, with wonderful swiftness, dropped to the ground and darted across the open space of a few yards, toward the creek. Side by side, with crests erect, they glided, and one of them still held between his jaws the unfortunate young sparrow. The boy did not hesitate a moment. Still making a great noise, but hoarsely for a creature of his age, he ran to head them off and barely passed them as they touched the water. He leaped in ahead of them and they were beside him in an instant. The water was up to his waist. He plunged deeper recklessly. With a cry of rage he struck at the serpent with the bird, and struck and struck again, blindly, still giving utterance to that odd sound, and with the fury of a young demon. The woman had reached the bank and stood, unknowing what to do, shrieking in maternal terror, while across the clearing a man was running. And then a fierce chance blow, delivered with all the strength of the maddened boy, alighted fairly, just below the head of the snake carrying away the bird, and in a second it was done for, floating, writhing down the stream with a broken neck, and its tiny prey loosened and drifting away beside it.

The mother gasped in relief, but only for a moment. The boy cast one glance at the floating reptile and the bird, and only one, then turned to the other serpent. It had almost reached the shore, and between that and the covert it might attain was a stretch of shrubless ground. Already its black length was defined on the short grass when the boy rushed from the water with uplifted club, just as his father came in full view of the scene from the other side. With cries like those of some young wild beast, the child ran at the snake, raining blows with the stout club, and with rage in every feature. The black-snake, checked in its course, turned with the constrictor's instinct and sprang at the boy, whipping its strong coils about one of its assailant's legs and rearing its head aloft to a level with his face. The boy but struck and gasped and stumbled over some obstruction, and, somehow, the snake was wrenched away, and then there was another rush at it, another rain of blows, and it was hit as had been its mate, and lay twisting with a broken back. The man dashed through the creek and came upon the scene with a great stick in his hand, but its use was not required. The only labor which devolved upon him was to tear away from his quarry the boy who was possessed of a spirit of rage and vengeance beyond all reasoning. Upon the heaving, tossing thing, so that he would have been fairly in its coils had it possessed longer any power, he leaped, striking fiercely and screaming out all the fearful terms he knew—what would have been the wildest of all abandonment of profanity had he but acquired the words for such performance. His father caught him by the arm, and he struggled with him. It was simply a young madman. Carried across the creek and held in bonds for a brief period, he suddenly burst out sobbing, and then went to inspect the ravished nest where the two old birds hovered mourningly about, and where the remaining nestlings seemed dead at first, though they subsequently recovered, so gruesomely had the fascination of their natural enemy affected them!

What happened then? What happens when any father and mother have occasion to consider the matter of a son, a child, bone of their bone and flesh of their flesh, who has transgressed some rule they have set up for him wisely, thoughtfully, but with no provision for emotional or extraordinary contingencies, because it would be useless, since he could not comprehend exceptions. They took him to the house. The father looked at him queerly, but with an expression that was far removed from anger on his face, and his mother took the young man aside and washed him, and put on another hickory shirt, and told him that his sparrows would raise a pretty good family after all, and that it wouldn't be so hard for the old birds to feed three as four.

Early that same evening a six-foot father strolled over to the place of the nearest settler, a mile or so away, and the two men walked back, talking together as neighbors will in a new country, though they do not so well in cities, and when they reached the creek one of them, the father, cut a forked twig and lifted the black-snake to its full length. Its head, raised even with his, allowed its tail to barely touch the ground.

Evidently the men were interested, and evidently one of them was rather proud of something. But he said nothing to his son about it. That would, in its full consideration, have involved a licking of somebody for disobedience of orders. It was a good thing for the bereaved song-sparrows, though. Older heads than that of the boy were now considerate of their welfare. Lucky sparrows were they!

As for the youth, he had, that night, queer dreams, which he remembered all his life. He was battling with the snakes again, and the fortunes of war shifted, and there was much trouble until daylight. Then, with the sun breaking in a blaze upon the clearing, with the ground and trees flashing forth illuminated dew-drops, with a clangor of thousands of melodious bird-voices—even the bereaved father song-sparrow was singing—he was his own large self again, and went forth conquering and to conquer. He found the murdered nestling stranded down the creek, and buried it with ceremony. He found both dead invaders, and punched their foul bodies with a long stick. And he wished a bear would come and try to take a pig!

This was the boy. This was the field he grew in, the nature of his emergence into active entity, and this may illustrate somewhat his unconscious bent as influenced by early surroundings, while showing some of the fixed features of heredity, for he came of a battling race.

CHAPTER IV

GROWING UP WITH THE COUNTRY

Have you ever seen a buckwheat field in bloom? Have you stood at its margin and gazed over those acres of soft eiderdown? Have your nostrils inhaled the perfume of it all, the heavy sweetness toned keenly with the whiff of pine from the adjacent wood? Have you noted the wild bees in countless myriads working upon its surface and gathering from each tiny flower's heart that which makes the clearest and purest and most wine-like of all honey? Have you stood at the forest's edge, perched high upon a fence, maybe of trees felled into a huge windrow when first the field was cleared, or else of rails of oak or ash, both black and white—the black ash lasts the longer, for worms invade the white—and looked upon a field of growing Indian corn, the green spread of it deep and heaving, and noted the traces of the forest's tax-collectors left about its margins: the squirrel's dainty work and the broken stalks and stripped ears upon the ground, leavings of the old raccoon, the small bear of the forest, knowing enough to become a friend of man when caught and tamed, and almost human in his ways, as curious as a scandal-monger and selfish as a money-lender?

Have you gone into the hard maple wood, the sugar bush, in early spring, the time of frosty nights and sunny days, and driven home the gouge and spile, and gathered the flowing sap and boiled it in such pots and kettles as later pioneers have owned, and gained such wildwood-scented product as no confectioner of the town may ever hope to equal? Have you lain beside some pond, a broadening of the creek above an ancient beaver-dam, at night, in mellowest midsummer, and watched the muskrats at their frays and feeding? Have you hunted the common wildcat, short-bodied demon, whose tracks upon the snow are discernible each winter morning, but who is so crafty, so gifted with some great art of slyness, that you may grow to manhood with him all about you, yet never see him in the sinewy flesh unless with dog and gun, and food and determination, you seek his trail, and follow it unreasoningly until you terminate the stolid quest with a discovery of the quarry lying close along the body of some eloping, stunted tree, and with a lively episode in immediate prospect? Did you ever chase a wolverine, last of his kind in a clearing-overflowed region, strange combination in character and form of bear and lynx, gluttonous and voracious, and strong and fearless, a beast descended almost unchanged from the time of the earliest cave-men, the horror of the bravest dog, and end his too uncivilized career with a rifle-shot at thoughtful distance?

Have you seen the wild pigeons, before pot-hunters invaded their southern roosts and breeding-grounds and slaughtered them by millions, exterminating one of the most wonderful of American game birds, sweep over in such dense clouds that the sun would be obscured, and at times so close to earth that a long pole thrust aloft from tree or hillock would stun such numbers as would make a gallant pot-pie? Have you followed the deer in the dense forest, clinging doggedly to his track upon the fresh snow from the dusk of early morning, startling him again and again from covert, and shooting whenever you caught even so much as a glimpse of his gray body through distant interstices of tree and brush, until, late in the afternoon, human endurance, which always surpasses that of the wild beast, overcame him, and he leaped less strongly with each new alarm and grew more reckless before twilight, and came within easy range and fed his enemies on the morrow? Have you watched for him beside the brackish waters of the lick, where, perched upon a rude, high scaffold built beside a tree, mosquito-bitten and uneasy, you waited and suffered, preserving an absolute silence and immobility until came ghost-like flitting figures from the forest to the shallow's edge, when the great gun, carrying the superstitious number of buckshot, just thirteen, roared out, awakening a thousand echoes of the night, and, clambering down, found a great antlered thing in its death agony?

Have you wandered through new clearings neglected for a season and waded ankle-deep in strawberry blooms, and, later, fed there upon such scarlet fruit, so fragrant and with such a flavor of its own that the scientific horticulturist owns to-day his weakness? Have you looked out upon the flats some bright spring morning and found them transformed into a shallow lake by the creek's first flood, and seen one great expanse of shining gold as the sun smote the thin ice made in the night but to disappear long before mid-day and leave a surface all ripples and shifting lights and shadows, upon which would come an occasional splash and great out-extending circles, as some huge mating pickerel leaped in his glee? Have you stood sometime, in sheer delight of it, and drawn into distended lungs the air clarified by hundreds of miles of sweep over an inland sea, the nearest shore not a score of miles away, and filtered through aromatic forests to your senses, an invisible elixir, exhilarating, without a headache as the price? Have you seen the tiger-lilies and crimson Indian-tobacco blossoms flashing in the lowlands? Have you trapped the mink and, visiting his haunts, noticed there the old blue crane flitting ever ahead of you through dusky corridors, uncanny, but a friend? Have you—but there are a thousand things!

If you have not seen or known or felt all these fair things—so jumbled together in the allusion here, without a natural sequence or thought or reason or any art—if you have not owned them all and so many others that may not here be mentioned, then you have missed something of the gifts and glories of growth in a new land. Such experience comes but to one generation. But one generation grows with the conquest, and it is a great thing. It is man-making.

And from the east came more hewers of wood, not drawers of water, and the axe swung all around, and new clearings were made and earlier ones broadened, and where fireweed first followed, the burning of the logs there were timothy and clover, though rough the mowing yet, and the State was "settled." Roads through the woods showed wagon-ruts, now well defined; houses were not so far apart, and about them were young orchards. The wild was being subjugated. The tame was growing. The boy was growing with it.

There was nothing particularly novel in the manner of this youth's development, save that, as he advanced in years, he became almost a young Indian in all woodcraft, and that the cheap, long, single-barreled shotgun, which was his first great personal possession, became, in his skilled hands, a deadly thing. Wild turkey and ruffed grouse, and sometimes larger game, he contributed to the family larder, and he had it half in mind to seek the remoter west when he grew older, and become a mighty hunter and trapper, and a slaughterer of the Sioux. The Chippewas of his own locality were scarcely to be shot at. Those remaining had already begun the unpretending life most of them live to-day, were on good terms with everybody, tanned buckskin admirably, and he approved of them. With the Sioux it was quite different. He had read of them in the weekly paper, which was now a part of progress, and he had learned something of them at the district school— for the district school had come, of course. It springs up in the United States after forests have been cut away, just as springs the wheat or corn. And the district school was, to the youth, a novelty and a vast attraction. It took him into Society.

Through forest paths and from long distances in each direction came the pupils to this first school of the region, and there were perhaps a score of them in all, boys and girls, and the teacher was a fair young woman from the distant town. The school-house was a structure of a single room, built in the wood, and squirrels dropped nuts upon its roof from overhanging boughs and peeped in at the windows, and sometimes a hawk would chase a fleeing bird into the place, where it would find a sure asylum, but create confusion. Once a flock of quail came marching in demurely at the open door, while teacher and pupils maintained a silence at the pretty sight. And once the place was cleared by an invasion of hornets enraged at something. That was a great day for the boys.

The studies were not as varied as in the cross-roads schools to-day. There was the primer, and there were a few of the old Webster spelling-books, but, while the stories of the boy in the apple tree and the overweening milkmaid were familiar, the popular spelling-book was Town's, and the readers were First, Second, Third and Fourth, and their "pieces" included such classics as "Webster's Reply to Hayne" and "Thanatopsis," and numerous clever exploits of S. P. Willis in blank verse. Davie's Arithmetic was dominant, and, as for grammar, whenever it was taught, Brown's was the favorite. There was, even then, in the rural curriculum the outlining of that system of the common schools which has made them of this same region unexcelled elsewhere in all the world. There were strong men, men who could read the future, controlling the legislation of some of the new States.

The studies mentioned, and geography were the duties now in hand, and there was indifference or hopefulness or rivalry among those of the little group as there is now in every school, from some new place in Oklahoma to old Oxford, over seas. In all scholarship, it chanced that this same boy, Grant Harlson, was easily in the lead. His mother, an ex-teacher in another and older State, loving, regardful, tactful, had taught him how to read and comprehend, and he had something of a taste that way and a retentive memory. So, inside the rugged schoolroom, he had a certain prestige. Outside, he took his chances.

CHAPTER V

GRIM-VISAGED WAR

It has been said that there were some twenty children in the school. They were of various degrees and fortunes. There were the sons and daughters of the land-owners, the pioneers, and there were the sons and daughters of the men who worked for them, mostly the drifting class, who occupied log houses on unclaimed ground and got flour or meal or potatoes for their services with the steadier or more masterful. In the school, though, there were no distinctions on this account. There were but two measurements of standing among girls and boys together, their relative importance in their classes, the teacher giving force to this, and among the boys alone the equation resulting from the issue of all personal encounter. Boys will be boys, and our fighting Anglo-Saxon blood will tell.

There were Harrison Woodell and George Appleton and Frank Hoadly and Mortimer Butler, among the older boys; and, among the second growth, though varying somewhat in their ages, were Alf Maitland and Maurice Shannon and Grant Harlson, and three or four others who ranked with them. The girls differed more in age, for there were some who aspired to be teachers, who, if boys, would have been home at work in summer-time, and some who could come, while very young, since their older sisters came with them to exercise all needed care. And among the smaller ones, though not so young as some, was Katie Welwood, a black-haired, black-eyed, evil-tempered little thing, who was the rage among the boys. She had smiled upon Grant Harlson, and smiled upon young Maitland, so early in her years is the female a coquette, and they looked askance upon each other, though they were the best of friends. Had they not together defied the big George Appleton, and vanquished him in running fight, and were they not sworn allies, come any weal or woe! But woman, even at the age of ten, has ever been the cause of trouble between males, and those two had, on her account, a mortal feud. It all came suddenly. There had been certain jealousies and heartaches caused by the raven-locked young vixen with the winning eyes, but there had been no outspoken words of anger between these vassals in her train until there came excuse in other way, for your country lad is modest, and never admits that his ailing has aught to do with the grand passion. But there had been a sharp debate over the proper ownership of a big gray squirrel at which they had shot their arrows from strong hickory bows together, and, with this excuse for fuel to the fire already smoldering, there soon came a great flame. Neither would yield to one he knew in his heart addicted to winning, villainously, the affections of the young woman, and so they fought. Unfortunately for Grant, Napoleon was at least in a measure right when he remarked that Providence always favored the heaviest battalions, and equally unfortunate for him that Alf, as resolute as he, was just a little heavier, was as tough of fiber at that stage of their young careers, and was, in a general way, what a patron of the prize ring would term the better man. Grant went home licked as thoroughly as any country boy, not hyper-critical, could ask, and should have felt that all was lost save honor. But he did not feel that way. He did not consider honor at greater length than is generally done by any boy of ten, on the way to eleven, but he did want vengeance. To lose his siren and a portion of his blood—"-'twas from the nose," as Byron says—together, was too much for his philosophy. He must have vengeance! He was no lambkin, and he knew things. He had read the Swiss Family Robinson. He resolved that on the morrow he would spear his hated rival and successful adversary!

CHAPTER VI

THE SPEARING OF ALFRED

"The spears they carried, though entirely of wood, were dangerous weapons," says the old writer in describing the armament of a tribe of the South Sea islanders. "Their points are hardened by being subjected to fire, and, in the hands of those fierce men, they are as deadly as the assegai of the African."

This passage, which he had stumbled upon somewhere, was of deepest interest to young Harlson. His armament, he felt, was not yet what it should be. He had arrived at the dignity of a gun, it was true, but that was quite another thing. What he needed was something especially adapted for personal encounter and for any knight-errantry which chanced to offer itself. He had imagined what might occur if he were with Katie Welwood and they should be assailed by anything or anybody. He had large ideas of what was a lover's duty, and was under the impression, from what he had read, that a proper knight should go always prepared for combat. So he had fashioned him a spear, a formidable weapon contrived with great exactitude after the South Sea island recipe. He had gone into the woods and selected a blue beech, straight as could be found, and nearly an inch in thickness. From this he had cut a length of perhaps ten feet, which, with infinite labor and risk of jack-knife, he had whittled down to smoothness and to whiteness. Upon one end he left as large a head as the sapling would allow, and this, after shaving it into the fashion of a spear-blade, he had plunged into the fire until it had begun to char. He had scraped away the charring with a piece of broken glass, and, as a result of his endeavors, had really a spear with a point of undoubted sharpness and great hardness. He took huge pride in his new weapon, and carried it to school with him for days and on his various woodland expeditions, but there had come no chance to rescue any distressful maiden anywhere, and the envy and admiration of the other boys had but resulted in emulation and in the appearance of similar warlike gear among them.

He had tired of carrying the thing about, and had for some time left it peacefully at home, leaning beside the hog-pen. Now all was different. The time had come! He would have revenge, and have it in a gory way. As the South Sea islanders treated their foes, his should be treated. He would go upon the war-path, and as for Alf—well, he was sorry for him in a general way, but all mercy was dead within his breast specifically. He remembered something in the reader:

"'Die! spawn of our kindred! Die! traitor to Lara!' As he spake, there was blood on the spear of Mudara!"

There must be blood, and he laid his plans with what he considered the very height of savage craft and ingenuity.

The father of Alf was a sturdy man and good one, but he had a weakness. He was the chief supporter in the neighborhood of the itinerant minister who exhorted throughout this portion of the country, and he had imbibed, perhaps, too much of a fancy for hearing himself talk at revival meetings, and for hearing himself in long prayers at home. His petitions covered a great range of subjects, and he was regular in their presentation. The family prayers before breakfast every morning were serious matters to the boys from one point of view, and not as serious as they should have been from another. Present, and kneeling at chairs about the room, they always were on these occasions, for the order was imperative, and the father's arm was strong, and above the door hung a strap of no light weight, constituting as it had once done that portion of a horse's harness known technically as the bellyband. So the boys were always there, each at his particular chair, and Grant Harlson, who had been present at these orisons many a time, knew exactly where Alf's chair was, and the attitude he must occupy. It was close beside an open window, and his back was always toward the opening, this particular attitude having been dictated by the father in the vain hope of making his buoyant offspring more attentive if their gaze were diverted from things outside. And all these circumstances the dreadful savage from the South Sea islands was considering with care. They are very regular in their habits in the country, and he knew just the moment when the morning devotions would begin—some fifteen minutes before the breakfast hour. He knew about how long he would be in traversing the distance between his own house and the scene of the coming tragedy, and the morning after his resolve was made he bolted his own breakfast in a hurry, seized his spear, and scurried down the wood road until he approached the verge of the Maitland clearing. Then began a series of extraordinary movements.

Mr. Maitland's house stood close by the wood at one side of the clearing, and Grant could easily have walked unperceived until within a few yards of the place, had he but kept hidden by the trees; but such was not his course. Right across the clearing, and passing near the house, had been dug a great ditch a yard in depth, a year or two before, with the intent of draining a piece of lowland lately subjugated. This ditch had been overgrown with weeds until it was almost hidden from sight, and now in summer time its bottom was but a sandy surface. It was with the aid of this natural shelter that the wily invader proposed to steal upon his enemy. Already he was lurking near its entrance.

Just why he had to "lurk" at this particular juncture Grant could not probably have told. There was not the slightest necessity for lurking. There were no windows in the side of the house toward him, and no one was visible about the place, but he knew what he had read, and he knew that the savages of the

South Sea islands were always addicted to lurking just previous to springing upon their unsuspecting victims, and he was bound to lurk and do it thoroughly. His manner of lurking consisted, before he reached the clearing fence, in crouching very low and creeping along in a most constrained and uncomfortable manner, occasionally dropping to the ground slowly and with utter noiselessness and rising again with equal caution. All this time the face of the young man wore what he conceived to be an expression of most bloody purpose craftily concealed. Upon reaching the fence, he shot his head above it, and withdrew it with lightning-like rapidity, frightening almost into convulsions, in her nest, a robin whose home was between the rails in the immediate vicinity. Of course he could have looked through the fence with greater ease, but that would have involved no such dramatic effect. His sudden view of the landscape taken, the boy climbed the fence, ran to the dry ditch, parted the overhanging weeds and leaped down. Once in the dry waterway, he was utterly concealed from view, even had any one been near; but that made no difference with his precautions. He knew that after savages had lurked, they always glided, and that what the writers describe as "a snake-like motion" was something absolutely essential.

Spear in hand and creeping on his hands and knees, the destroyer advanced along the drain, lying flat and wriggling with much patience wherever a particularly clear stretch of sand presented itself. Half way across the field he raised his head with a movement so slow that a full minute was occupied in the performance, parted the weeds gently and peered out to get his bearings and ascertain if any foemen were in sight. There were no foemen, and his progress had been satisfactory. The remainder of the desperate advance was made with no less adroitness and success. At last there fell upon the ear of the avenger the sound of a human voice. He was close to the house, and the morning exercises had begun!

Here was the moment for the exhibition of all South Sea island craft, and the moment was about at hand, too, for exhibition of the full measure of a South Sea islander's ferocity! The islander glided from the ditch, crept to the house and slowly put forth his head until he could see around the corner. There, within three feet of him, back to the window, kneeling beside his chair, was Alf, ostensibly paying deep attention to his father's unctuous and sonorous sentences, though really, as Grant could see, engaged in flicking kernels of corn at his brother in another corner. His jeans trousers were, as a result of his present attitude, drawn tightly across that portion of his body nearest to the window, and never fairer mark was offered savage spear! Not a moment did the avenger hesitate. He poised his weapon, took deadly aim, and lunged!

Never was quiet of a summer morning broken more suddenly and startlingly. A yell so loud, so wild, so blood-curdling, ascended from within the farm-house, that even nature seemed to shiver for a moment. Then came the rush of feet and the clamor of many voices. Out of doors ran all the household, the father included, so appalling had been Alf's cry of apparently mortal agony, to learn the source of all the trouble. There was nothing to be seen. Not a living being was in sight. It dawned upon the elders gradually that nothing very serious had occurred, and the father and the females of the household went in to breakfast, the exercises of the morning not being now renewed, while Alf and his brother scoured the wood. Upon one leg of Alf's jeans trousers appeared an artistic dab of red. He had been wounded, and for days the sitting down and the uprising of him would be acts of care.

And where was the South Sea islander? Almost as he lunged he had leaped backward around the corner of the house and run for the covered ditch. Once in that covert, he did not "lurk" to any great extent. He crawled away as rapidly as his hands and knees would carry him, reasoning that the boys would, upon finding no one near the house, run naturally to the wood in search of the enemy. They never thought of the old ditch, though, later in the day, the thing occurred to them, and an examination of the sandy bottom told the story. The edge of the field was reached, the islander lying very low until he could climb the fence in safety. Then he examined his fatal spear-point. It appeared incarnadined. There was certainly blood on the spear of Mudara!

A week later Alf caught Grant, and, despite another valiant struggle, licked him mercilessly. A year later the fortunes of war had turned the other way. As they grew, these boys, like race-horses well-matched, passed each other, physically, time and again, one now surging to the front and then another, with no great difference at any time between them.

CHAPTER VII

HOW FICTION MADE FACT

What may become a streak of proper modern chivalry in the man is but a fantastic imagining in the boy. Some one has said that but for the reading of "Ivanhoe" in the South, there would have been no war of the rebellion, that the sentiment of knightliness and desire to uphold opinions in material encounter was so fostered by the presence of the book in thousands of households that, when the issue came, a majority was for war which might have been otherwise inclined under more practical teaching. This may or may not have been the case. There would be nothing strange in it were the theory correct; the influence of great novels is always underrated; but certain it is that the reading of the age influences much the youth, and that many a bent of mind is made by the books that lie about the house when some strong young intellect is forming. So with this boy. The same force which made of him a great savage marauder of the South Sea islands, though modified by a keener perception and a broader intelligence, affected him as he grew older. There were a few books available to him; and what a reader he was, and what a listener! His father would sometimes read aloud at night from current weeklies, and then the boy would sprawl along the floor, his feet toward the great fireplace, his head upon a rolled-up sheepskin, and drink in every word. "East Lynne" was running as a serial then, and he would have given all his worldly possessions to have had Sir Francis Levison alone in the wood, and had his spear, and at his back some half-dozen of the boys whom he could name. In some publication, too, at about that time, appeared the tale of the adventures of Captain Gardiner and Captain Daggett in antarctic wastes, seeking the sea-lions' skins, and the story of pluckiness and awful trial affected his imagination deeply. Years afterward, when he himself was at death's portal once, because of a grievous injury, and when ice was bound upon his head to keep away the fever from his brain, he imagined in his delirium that he was Captain Gardiner, and called aloud the orders to the crew which he had heard read when a boy, and which had so long lain in his memory's storehouse among the unconsidered lumber.

The boy's reading included all there was in his home, and the small collection was not a bad one. "Chambers' Miscellany" was in the accidental lot, and good for him it was. "Chambers' Miscellany" is better reading than much that is given to the world to-day, and the boy rioted in the adventure-flavored tales and sketches. Scott's poetical works were there, and Shakespeare, but the latter was read only for the story of the play, and "Titus Andronicus" outranked even "Hamlet" among the tragedies. As for Scott, the stirring rhymes had marked effect, and this had one curious sequence. Tales of the lance and tilting have ever captivated boys, and Grant was no exception. Alf did not read so much, was of a nature less imaginative, and his younger brother, Valentine, read not at all, but among them was enacted a great scene of chivalry which ended almost in a tragedy. Grant, his mind absorbed in jousting and its laurels, explained the thing to Alf and induced him to read the tales of various encounters. Alf was more or less affected by the literature and ready to do his share toward making each of them a proper warrior fit for any fray. They considered the situation with much earnestness, and concluded that the only way to joust was to joust, and that Valentine should act as marshal of the occasion, for a marshal at a tourney, they discovered, was a prime necessity. As for coursers, barbs, destriers, or whatever name their noble steeds might bear, they had no choice. There were but a couple of clumsy farm mares available to them, and these the knights secured, their only equipments being headstalls abstracted from the harness in the barn, while the course fixed upon was a meadow well out of sight from the houses and the eyes of the elders. Valentine was instructed in his duties, particularly in the manner of giving the word of command. *Laissez aller*, as found in "Ivanhoe," Grant did not understand, but a passage from "The Lady of the Lake":

"Now, gallants! for your ladies' sake, Upon them with the lance!"

seemed to answer every purpose, and Valentine was instructed to commit it to memory, as the event proved, with but indifferent success. He comprehended, in a vague way, that the warriors were to do battle for the honor of their true loves, but, at the critical moment, the lines escaped him and he had to improvise. The lances were rake-handles, and, as this was not to be a fray *a l'outrance*, about the end of each formidable weapon was wadded and tied an empty flour bag.

The unwilling, lumbering mares were brought upon the ground, and Valentine held the headstall reins while a preliminary ceremony was performed, for your perfect knight omits no courteous detail. Gloves were unknown about the farm, but Grant drew from his pocket a buckskin mitten, and with it slapped Alf suddenly in the face. It was to be regretted that the aggressor had somewhat exaggerated the mediaeval glove idea, and had not previously explained to Alf that to fling one's glove in a foeman's face was one proper form of deadly insult preceding mortal combat, for, ignoring lances, steeds and all about them, the assailed personage immediately "clinched," and the boys rolled over in a struggle, earnest, certainly, but altogether commonplace. It was with the greatest difficulty, while defending himself, that Grant was enabled to explain that his act was one rendered necessary by the laws of chivalry and a part of the preliminaries of the occasion, instead of an attack in cold blood upon an unwarned adversary. Alf accepted the apology gloweringly, and manifested great anxiety to secure his lance, and mount. It was evident the encounter would be deadly.

Some hundred yards apart, with the perplexed, astonished old mares facing each other, sat the warriors in their saddles, or, rather, in the place where their saddles would have been had they possessed them. Each grasped the headstall reins firmly in his left hand, and with his right aimed his top-heavy lance in a somewhat wobbling manner at his adversary. It must soon be known to all the world of knighthood which was the grimmer champion! At middle distance and well to one side, stood Grand Marshal Valentine, racking his brains for the lines which should give the signal for the shock, but all in vain. Desperation gave him inspiration. "Let 'er go for your girls!" he roared.

Never, even in the gentle and joyous passage of arms at Ashby, or on the Field of the Cloth of Gold, was afforded a more thrilling spectacle than when these two paladins rushed to the onset and met in mid-career. Each gave a yell and dug his heels into his charger, and whacked her with the butt end of his lance, and forced her into a ponderous gallop for the meeting. It matters not now what was the precise intent of either jouster, which of them aimed at gorget or head-piece, or at shield, for—either because the flour bags made the lances difficult to manage or of some unevenness in the ground— each missed his enemy in the encounter! Not so the two old mares! They came together with a mighty crash and rolled over in a great cloud of dust and grass and mane and tail and boy and spear and flour-bag!

There is a providence that looks after reckless youth especially, else there would have been broken bones, or worse; but out of the confusion two warriors scrambled to their feet, dazed somewhat and dirty, but unharmed, and two old mares floundered into their normal attitude a little later, evidently much disgusted with the entire proceeding. And Valentine, grand marshal, who had chanced to have a little difficulty with his elder brother the day before, promptly awarded the honors of the tournament to Grant on the ground that old Molly, the horse ridden by Alfred, seemed a little more shaken up than the other.

Of course there were other books than those of chivalric doings which appealed to this young reader so addicted to putting theory into practice at all risks. "Robinson Crusoe," and Byron, and D'Aubigne's "History of the Reformation," and "Midshipman Easy," and "Snarleyow," and the "Woman in White," "John Brent," and Josephus, and certain old readers, such as the American First Class Book, made up the odd country library, and there was not a book in the lot which was not in time devoured. There was another book, a romance entitled "Don Sebastian," to which at length a local tragedy appertained. The scene was laid in Spain or Portugal and the hero of the story was a very gallant character, indeed, one to be relied upon for the accomplishment of great slaughter in an emergency, but who was singularly unlucky in his love affair, in the outcome of which Grant became deeply interested, too deeply, as the event proved. Upon the country boy of eleven or twelve devolve always, in a new country, certain responsibilities not unconnected with the great fuel question,—the keeping of the wood-box full,—and these duties, in the absorption of the novel, the youth neglected shamefully. A casual allusion or two, followed by a direct announcement of what must come, had been entirely lost upon him, and, one day, as he was lying by the unreplenished fire, deep in the pages of the book, the volume was lifted gently from his hands, and, to his horror, dropped upon the blazing coals against the back-log. Many things occurred to him in later life of the sort men would avoid, but never came much greater mental shock than on that black occasion. Stunned, dazed, he went outside and threw himself upon the grass and tried to reason out what could be done. Was he never to know the fate of Don Sebastian? It was beyond endurance! A cheap quality of literature the book was, no doubt, but he was not critical at that age, and in later years he often sought the volume out of curiosity to learn what in his boyhood had entranced him, but he never found it. It was a small, fat volume, very like a pocket Bible in shape, bound cheaply in green cloth, and printed in England, probably somewhere in the '30's, but it had disappeared. The bereaved youth was, henceforth, in as sore a retrospective strait over "Don Sebastian" as Mr. Andrew Lang declares he is, to-day, with his "White Serpent" story.

Byron—"Don Juan," in particular—had an effect upon the youth, and "The Prisoner of Chillon" gave him dreams. "Snarleyow" was the book, though, which struck him as something great in literature. The demon dog tickled his fancy amazingly. He was somewhat older when he read "Jane Eyre" and "John Brent," and could recognize a little of their quality, but "Snarleyow" came to him at an age when there was nothing in the world to equal it.

Meanwhile the whole face of nature was changing, and the boy was necessarily keeping up with the procession of new things. Broad meadows were where even he, a mere boy still, had seen dense woodland; there were highways, and it was far from the farmhouse door to the forests edge. The fauna had diminished. The bear and wolverine had gone forever. The fox rarely barked at night; the deer and wild turkey were far less plentiful, though the ruffed grouse still drummed in the copses, and the quail whistled from the fences. Different, even, were the hunters in their methods. The boy, whose single-barreled shot-gun had known no law, now carried a better piece, and scorned to slay a sitting bird. Both he and Alf became great wing shots, and clever gentlemen sportsmen from the city who sometimes came to hunt with them could not hope to own so good a bag at the day's end. Wise as to dogs and horses were they, too, and keen riders at country races. And ridges of good muscles stiffened now their loins, and their chests were deepening, and at "raisings," when the men and boys of the region wrestled after their work was done, the two were not uncounted. For them the country school had accomplished its mission. The world's geography was theirs. Grammar they had memorized, but hardly comprehended. As for mathematics, they were on the verge of algebra. Then came the force of laws of politics and trade, a shifting of things, and Grant strode out of nature to learn the artificial. His family was removed to town.

Western, or rather Northwestern, town life, when the town has less than ten thousand people, varies little with the locality. There is the same vigor everywhere, because conditions are so similar. It is odd, too, the close resemblance all through the great lake region in the local geography of the towns. Small streams run into larger ones, and these in turn enter the inland seas, or the straits, called rivers, which connect them. Where the small rivers enter the larger ones, or where the larger enter the straits or lakes, men made the towns. These were the water cross-roads, the intersections of nature's highways, and so it comes that to so many of these towns there is the great blue water front intersected at its middle by a river. There is a bridge in the town's main street, and the smell of water is ever in the air. Boys learn to swim like otters and skate like Hollanders, and their sisters emulate them in the skating, though not so much in the wimming as they should. There is a life full of great swing. The touch between the town and country is exceedingly close, and the country family which comes to the community blends swiftly with the current. So with the family of Grant Harlson and so with him personally. A year made him collared and cravatted, short-cropped of hair, mighty in high-school frays, and with a new ambition stirring him, of a quality to compare with that of one Lucifer of unbounded reputation and doubtful biography. There was something beyond all shooting and riding and wrestling fame and the breath of growing things. There was another world with reachable prizes and much to feed upon. He must wear medals, metaphorically, and eat his fill, in time.

The high-school is really the first telescope through which a boy so born and bred looks fairly out upon this planet. The astronomer who instructs him is often of just the sort for the labor, a being also climbing, one not to be a high-school principal forever, but using this occupation merely as a stepping-stone upon his ascending journey. If he be conscientious, he instils, together with his information that all Gaul is divided and that a parasang is not something to eat, also the belief that the game sought is worth the candle, and that hard study is not wasted time. Such a teacher found young Harlson; such a teacher was Professor—they always call the high-school principal "Professor" in small towns—Morgan, and he took an interest in the youth, not the interest of the typical great educator, but rather that of an older and aspiring jockey aiding a younger one with his first mount, or of a railroad engineer who tells his fireman of a locomotive's moods and teaches him the tricks of management. They might help each other some day. Well equipped, too, was Morgan for the service. No shallow graduate of some mere diploma-manufactory, but one who believed in the perfection of means for an end,—an advocate of thoroughness.

So it came that for four years Grant Harlson studied feverishly,—selfishly might be almost the word,—such was the impulse that moved him under Morgan's teaching, and so purely objective all his reasoning. In his vacations he hunted, fished, and developed the more thews and sinews, and acquired new fancies as to whether an Irish setter or a Gordon made the better dog with woodcock, and upon various other healthful topics, but his main purpose never varied. In his classes there were fair girls, and in high-schools there is much callow gallantry; but at this period of his life he would have none of it. He was not timid, but he was absorbed. Morgan told him one day that he was ready for college.

CHAPTER VIII

NEW FORCES AT WORK

"You will be kind enough, sir, to write upon the blackboard two couplets:

"What do you *think* I'll shave you for nothing and *give you a drink*."

"And "*What* do you think I'll shave you for *nothing* and give you a drink."

"You will observe that, while the wording is the same, the inflection is different. Please punctuate them properly, and express the idea I intend to convey."

This from a professor, keen-eyed and unassuming in demeanor, to a big, long-limbed young fellow, facing, with misgivings despite himself, a portion of the test of whether or not he were qualified for admission as a freshman into one of our great modern universities. He had not been under much apprehension until the moment for the beginning of the trial. There was now to be met the first issue in the new field. He plunged into his task.

Then the professor:

"Well, yes, you have caught my idea. How write upon the board: 'This is the forest primeval,' and a dozen lines or so following, from this slip. Scan that for me; parse it; show me the relations of words and clauses, and all that sort of thing."

A pause; some only half-confident explanation, and enlargement upon the subject by the young man.

The professor again:

"H-u-u-m—well—now you may write—no, you needn't—just tell me the difference, in your opinion, between what are known as conjunctions and prepositions. Say what you please. We ask no odds of them. Be utterly free in your comment."

More explanations by the young man. The professor: "We'll not pursue that subject. You might tell us, incidentally, what a trochaic foot is?—Yes.—And who wrote that 'Forest primeval' you just scanned?—Certainly—That will do, I think. Oh, by the way, who was Becky Sharp?—The most desirable woman in 'Vanity Fair,' eh? I may be half inclined to agree with you, but I was asking who, not what. Good afternoon. You have passed your examination in English literature. I trust you may be equally successful in other departments. Good afternoon, sir."

And this was all from a professor whose name was known on more than one continent and who was counted one of the greatest of educators. Such was his test of what of English literature was required in a freshman. A lesser man than this great teacher would have taken an hour for the task and learned less, for, after all, did not the examination cover the whole ground? The droll range of the inquiry was such that the questioner had gauged, far better than by some more ponderous and detailed system, the quality of the young man's knowledge in one field. One of the strong teachers this, one not afraid of a departure, and one of those who, within the last quarter of a century, have laid the foundations of new American universities deep and wide, and given to the youth facilities for a learning not creed-bound, nor school-bound, but both liberal and of all utility.

It was well for the particular freshman whose examination is here described that his first experience with a professor was with such a man. It gave confidence, and set him thinking. With others of the examiners he did not, in each instance, fare so happily. What thousands of men of the world there are to-day who remember with something like a shudder still the inquisition of Prof. —, whose works on Greek are text-books in many a college; or the ferocity of Prof. —, to whom calculus was grander than Homer! But the woes of freshmen are passing things.

What Grant Harlson did in college need not be told at any length. He but plucked the fruit within his reach, not over-wisely in some instances, yet with some industry. He had, at least, the intelligence to feel that it is better to know all of some things than a little of all things, and so surpassed, in such branches as were his by gift and inclination, and but barely passed in those which went against the mental grain.

It may be the professor of English literature had something to do with this. Between Grant and him there grew up a friendship somewhat unusual under all the circumstances. One day the professor was overtaken by the student upon a by-way of the campus, and asked some questions regarding certain changed hours of certain recitations, and, having answered, detained the questioner carelessly in general conversation. The elder became interested—perhaps because it was a relief to him to talk with such a healthy animal—and, at the termination of the interview, invited him to call. There grew up rapidly, binding these two, between whose ages a difference of twenty years existed, a friendship which was never broken, and which doubtless affected to an extent the student's ways, for he at least accepted suggestions as to studies and specialties. This relationship resulted naturally in transplanting to the mind of the youth some of the fancies and, possibly, the foibles of the man. One incident will illustrate.

The student, during a summer vacation, had devoted himself largely to the copying of Macaulay's essays, for, in his teens, one is much impressed by the rolling sentences of that great writer. Upon his return Harlson told of his summer not entirely wasted, and expressed the hope that he might have absorbed some trifle of the writer's style.

The professor of English literature laughed.

"Better have taken Carlyle's 'French Revolution' or any one of half a dozen books which might be named. Let me tell a little story. Some time ago a fellow professor of mine was shown by a Swedish servant girl in his employ a letter she had just written, with the request that he would correct it. He found nothing to correct. It was a wonderfully clear bit of epistolary literature. He was surprised, and questioned the girl. He learned that, though well educated, she knew but little English, and had sought the dictionary, revising her own letter by selecting the shortest words to express the idea. Hence the letter's strength and clearness. Stick to the Saxon closely. Macaulay will wear off in time." And this was better teaching than one sometimes gets in class.

This is no tale of the inner life of an American university. It is but a brief summary of young Harlson's ways there. But some day, I hope, a Thomas Hughes will come who will write the story, which can be made as healthful as "Tom Brown," though it will have a different flavor. What a chance for character study! What opportunity for an Iliad of many a gallant struggle! Valuable only in a lesser degree than what is learned from books is what is learned from men in college, that is, from young men, and herein lies the greater merit of the greater place. In the little college, however high the grade of study, there is a lack of one thing broadening, a lack of acquaintance with the youth of many regions. The living together of a thousand hailing from Maine or California, or Oregon or Florida, or Canada or England, young men of the same general grade and having the same general object, is a great thing for them all. It obliterates the prejudice of locality, and gives to each the key-note of the region of another. It builds up an acquaintance among those who will be regulating a land's affairs from different vantage-grounds in years to come, and has its most practical utility in this. When men meet to nominate a President this fact comes out most strongly. The man from Texas makes a combination with the man from Michigan, and two delegations swing together, for have not these two men well known each other since the day their classes met in a rush upon the campus twenty years ago?

No studious recluse was Harlson. His backwoods training would not allow of that. In every class encounter, in every fray with townsmen, it is to be feared in almost every hazing, after his own gruesome experience—for they hazed then vigorously —he was a factor, and beefsteak had been bound upon his cheek on more than one occasion. A rollicking class was his, though not below the average in its scholarship, and the sometimes reckless mood of it just suited him. "There were three men of Babylon, of Babylon, of Babylon."

There is what some claim is an aristocracy in American colleges. It is asserted that the leading Greek fraternities are this, and that the existence of Alpha Delta Phi, Psi Upsilon or Delta Kappa Epsilon, or others of the secret groups, is not a good thing for the students as a whole. Yet in the existence of these societies is forged another of the links of life to come outside, and all the good things to be gained in college are not the ratings won in classes. Harlson was one of those with badges and deep in college politics. He never had occasion to repent it.

And so, with study, some rough encounter and much scheming and much dreaming, time passed until the world outside loomed up again at close quarters. The present view was a new struggle. The great money question intervened. There had come a blight upon his father's dollar crop, and when Grant Harlson left the university he was so nearly penniless that the books he owned were sold to pay his railroad fare.

CHAPTER IX

MRS. POTIPHAR

It must have been some person aged, say, twenty, who expressed to Noah the opinion that there wasn't going to be much of a shower. At twenty tomorrow is ever a clear day, and notes are easy things to meet, and friends and women are faithful, and Welsh rarebit is digestible, and sleep is rest, and air is ever good to breathe. Grant Harlson was not particularly troubled by the condition of his finances. That the money available had lasted till his schooling ended, was, at least, a good thing, and, as for the future, was it not his business to attend to that presently? Meanwhile he would dawdle for a week or two.

So the young man stretched his big limbs and lounged in hammocks and advised or domineered over his sisters, as the case might be, and read in a desultory way, and fished and shot, and ate with an appetite which threatened to bring famine to the family. Your lakeside small town is a fair place in July. He would loaf, he said, for a week or two. The loafing was destined to have character, perhaps to change a character.

There had come to Harlson in college, as to most young men, occasional packages from home, and in one of these he had found a pretty thing, a man's silk tie, worked wonderfully in green and gold, and evidently the product of great needlecraft. It was to his fancy, and he had thought to thank whichever of his sisters had wasted such time upon him, but had forgotten it when next he wrote, and so the incident had passed.

One day, wearing this same tie, he bethought him of his negligence lying supine on the grass, while his sister Bess was meanwhile reading in the immediate vicinity. He would be grateful, as a brother should.

"I say, Bess," he called, "I forgot to write about this tie and thank you. Which of you did it?"

Bess looked up, interested.

"I thought I wrote you when I sent the other things. None of us did it. It ws Mrs. Rolfston."

"Mrs. Rolfston?"

"Certainly. She was here one day, when we were making up a lot of things for you, and said that she'd make something herself to go with the next lot. A week or two later she brought me that tie, and I inclosed it. Pretty, isn't it?"

"Very pretty."

The young man on the grass was thinking.

He knew Mrs. Rolfston slightly; knew her as the wife of a well-to-do man who saw but little of her husband.

Daughter of a poor man of none too good character in the little town, she had grown up shrewd, self-possessed, and with much animal beauty. At twenty she had married a man of fifty, a builder of steamboats, a red-faced, riotous brute, who had bought her as he would buy a horse, and to whom she went easily because she wanted the position money gives. Within a week he had disgusted her to such an extent that she almost repented of the bargain. Within a year, he had tired of her and was openly unfaithful in every port upon the lakes, a vigorous, lawless debauchee. His ship-building was done in a distant port, and he rarely visited his wife. He rather feared her, mastiff as he was, for here was the keener intelligence, and her moods, at times, were desperate as his. So he furnished her abundant income and was content to let it go at that. It pleased her, also, to have it that way.

Harlson thought of the woman, and wondered somewhat. Black-haired, black-eyed, white-skinned, deep of bust and with a graceful and powerful swing of movement, she was a woman, physically considered, not of the common herd. She was a lioness, yet not quite the grand lioness of the desert. She lacked somewhat of dignity and grandeur of countenance, and had more of alertness and of craft. She was, though dark, more like the tawny beast of the Rocky Mountains, the California lion, as that great cougar is called, supple, full of moods and passion, and largely cat-like. She had filled his eye casually. Why had she sent him the tie, the silken thing in green and gold?

He thought and pulled his long limbs together and rose till he was sitting, and decided that it was but courteous, but his duty as a gentleman, to wander over to her house and thank her for her remembrance of him. It was but an expression of good will toward the family generally, this little act of hers; he knew that, but it was a personal matter, after all, and he should thank her. It was well to be thoughtful, to attend to the small amenities, and it took him more than the usual time to dress. His apparently careless summer garb required the adjustment of an expert here and there. He was an hour in the doing of it. When he emerged he was not, taken in a comprehensive way, bad-looking. He was clear-faced, strong-featured and of stalwart build.

The ordinary man he would not have feared in any meeting; of the woman he was about to meet he had some apprehension. He knew her quality, but—she had worked for him a tie! He went up the broad path to the doorway, between flowers and trees and shrubbery. It was three o'clock in the afternoon, and he would find her alone, he thought, for chances of calls are not so great in the smaller towns as in the cities; there is an average to be maintained, and Mrs. Jones or Mrs. Smith does not receive on days particularized. He was compelled to wait in the parlor but a moment. She came in, and he saw her for the first time in two years.

What a gift women have in producing physical effects upon the creature male, no matter what the woman's status. Mrs. Rolfston came in with a look of half inquiry on her face and with a presentation of herself which was perfect in its way. She wore some soft and fluffy dress—a man cannot describe a garb in detail—with that lace-surrounded triangular bareness upon the bosom just below the chin which is as irreproachable as it is telling. There was a relation between the swing of her drapery and, the movements of her body. She was rich of figure, and flexile. And she was glad to see Mr. Harlson, and said so. He was not really embarrassed. The time had passed when that could be his way. But he was puzzled as to what to say. Some comment he made upon the quality of the season and upon Mrs. Rolfston's appearance of good health. Then he entered upon his subject with no link of connection with preceding sentences. "I but learned to-day," he said, "that the tie I wear was made by you. All fellows have little fancies, I suppose. I have, anyhow. I liked this, though I did not know who made it. My sister told me, and I have come to thank you. Why did you do it for me?"

That was putting the case plainly enough, certainly, and promptly enough, but it was not of a nature to trouble Mrs. Rolfston. This was a clever woman, married ten years, and of experiences which varied. She even glanced over the visitor from head to heel before she answered, and her color deepened and her eyes brightened, though he did not note it.

"You have changed," she commented. "I should hardly have known you but for your lips and eyes. You are broader and taller, and a big man, are you not? How long do you stay in town? Will you spend the summer here?"

"I wish I could," he answered. "It is pleasant here, but I must work, you know. I may idle for a little time. You haven't said anything about the tie."

"Oh, the tie? Don't speak of that. I had the whim to make something for somebody—I have an embroidering mania on me sometimes—and there was a chance to dispose of it, you see."

The young man's face fell a little as he looked upon the great, handsome woman and heard her seemingly careless words. He did not want to go away, yet what excuse was there for staying? He rose, hat in hand.

Here, now, was the woman in a quandary. She had not anticipated such abruptness.

"Don't go yet," she said, impetuously. "I want to talk with you. Tell me all about the college, and yourself, and your plans. And—-about the tie—I wouldn't have made one for any one else. I remembered your face. You know I was go often at your home, and I wondered how it would suit you. You should take that interest as a compliment. And I am lonesome here, and you are idling, you say, and why should we not be good friends for the summer? The men in town annoy me, and the girls here are not bright enough for you. Let us be cronies, will you not? Take me fishing to-morrow. I want you to teach me how to catch bass in the river. I heard some one say once you knew better than any one else how that is done. Is not this a good idea of mine? It will help both of us kill time."

She sat there on the sofa, half stretched out, yet not carelessly nor ungracefully, but in an assumed laziness of real felini-shness, a woman just ten years older than the man she was addressing, yet in all the lushness of magnificent womanhood, and emanating all magnetism.

Harlson said he would call for her and that they would go fishing. And they went.

The light is tawny upon the lily-pods in shady places on the river. And rods, such as are used for bass, are light upon the wrist, and, in the lazy hours of mid-afternoon, when bass bite rarely, demand but slight attention. And two people idling in a boat get very close in thought together and come soon to know each other well. And a ruthless young man of twenty and a tempestuous woman of thirty are as the conventional tow and tinder.

And there were books she had never read in Mrs. Rolfston's library—for she was not a woman of books—which interested Harlson, and it was easier to read them there than take them home. And Mrs. Rolfston waited upon him—how gifted is a woman of thirty—and he felt bands upon him, and liked it, and would not reason to himself concerning it.

And one night, late, came a panting servant—Mrs. Rolfston had no men, only two women domestics, with her in her home—to say that her mistress had heard some one evidently attempting to open a window on the piazza, and that they were all in fear of their lives, and that she had fled out of the back way to ask Mr. Harlson the elder, or his son, to come over at once and look around.

The father laughed, and said that, had there been a burglar, he must have fled already, and the young man, laughing too, said that some one must go anyhow, in all courtesy to defenseless women, and that if Mrs. Rolfston feared for her front porch, he would lie upon a blanket in the lawn beside it to set her mind at rest. He had not slept beneath the stars alone, he said, since the family had left the farm. And there was much laughing, and Harlson took home the servant girl, and she, growing bold as they approached the house, ran up the path ahead of him. The lawn between the better house and street in the lake country town is often a little forest, so dense the trees and their foliage. And added to the fragrance of the leaves in later midsummer are the mingled odors of petunias and pinks and rosemary and bergamot and musk, for all these flourish late. And the moon comes through the tree-tops in splashes, and there is a softness and a shade, and it is all like a scented garden in some old Arabian story, and the senses are affected and, maybe, the reason. Harlson went up the path, half dreaming, yet alive in every vein. There was no burglar visible, but a wonderful woman, in fleecy dishabille, was sure she had heard a sound most sinister, and endangered women must be guarded of the strong.

And Grant Harlson returned not home that night; yet the moon, shining through the trees, revealed no form upon a blanket in the garden.

And the summer days drifted by; and the young man fresh from college, full of ambitions and dreams, found himself a creature he had never known, a something conscience-stricken, yet half-abandoned, and with a leaden weight upon his feet to keep them from carrying him away from the temptation.

He would force himself to a solitary day at times, and go out into the country with dog and gun, and tramp for miles, and wonder at himself. He had all sorts of fancies. He thought of his wickedness and his wasted time, and compared himself with the great men in the books who had been in similar evil straits,—with Marc Antony, with King Arthur in Gwendolen's enchanted castle, and with Geraint the strong but slothful, —rather far-fetched this last comparison,—and of all the rest. It was a grotesque variety, but amid it all he really suffered. And he would make good resolves and, for the moment, firm ones, and return to town when the dew was falling and the moonlight coming, and the tale was but retold. And the woman was wise, as women are, and conscienceless, yet suffering a little, too.

She had found more than a summer's toy, and she had grown to fear the great boy in his moods, and to want to keep him, and to doubt the measure of her art. This must be a hard thing, too, for such splendid pirates to bear. They may not even scuttle all the craft they capture.

Stanley Waterloo

And the root of all evil is sometimes the root of all good. The dollar pulls all ways. Harlson must earn his way. One day his father dropped a chance word regarding some one, miles in the country, who wanted a fence built inclosing a tract out of the wood. It was isolated work, a task of a month or two for a strong man, a mere laborer. Young Harlson became interested.

"Why shouldn't I try it?" he asked.

His father laughed.

"It's work for a toughened man, my boy. You have softened with six years of only study."

The boy laughed as well.

"You needn't fear," he said. "All strength is not attained upon a farm, and I want to swing an ax and maul again."

And that day he set out afoot for the home of the man who needed a fence. He told Mrs. Rolfston briefly. She paled a trifle, but made no objection. He said he would make visits to the town.

CHAPTER X

THE BUILDING OF THE FENCE

An ax, a maul, a yoke of oxen; these are the great requisites for him who would build a rail fence through a forest. Grant Harlson made the bargain for the work, hired a yoke of oxen, as you may do in the country, and secured the right to eat plain food three times a day at the cabin of a laborer. A bed he could not have, but the right to sleep in a barn back in the field, and there also to house his oxen for the night, was given him. He slept upon the hay-mow. He went into the forest and began his work. The wood was dense, and what is known all through the region as a black ash swale, lowland which once reclaimed from nature makes, with its rich deposits, a wondrous meadow-land. He "lined" the fence's course and cleared the way rudely through the forest, a work of days, and then he made the maul.

The mace of the mediaeval knight is the maul of to-day. No longer it cracks heads or helmets, but there is work for it. And it has developed into a mighty weapon. There are two sorts of maul in the lake country. As the stricken eagle is poetically described as supplying the feather for the arrow by which itself was hurt to death, the trees furnish forth the thing to rend them. Upon the side of the curly maple, aristocrat of the sugar bush, grows sometimes a vast wart. This wart has neither rhyme nor reason. It has no grain defined. It is twisted, convoluted, a solid, tough and heavy mass, and hard, almost, as iron. It is sawed away from the trunk with much travail, and is seasoned well, and from it is fashioned a great head, into which is set a hickory handle, and the thing will crush a rock if need be. This is the maul proper.

There is another maul, or mace, made from a cut of heavy iron-wood, a foot in length and half a foot in thickness, with the hickory handle set midway between iron bands, sprung on by the country blacksmith. This is sometimes called the beetle.

The beetle is a monster hammer, the maul a monster mace. Each serves its purpose well, but the beetle never has the swing and mighty force of the great heavy maple knot. Grant Harlson bought a seasoned knot of an old woodman and shaped a maul. He had learned the craft in youth.

The ash trees fell beneath the ax, the trunks were cut to rail lengths, and the oxen dragged logs through muck and mire and brush and bramble to the line of fence, and there the maul swung steadily in great strokes upon the iron and wooden wedges, the smell of timber newly split was in the air, and the heavy rails were lifted, and the fence began its growth.

And it was lonesome in the depths of the wood, for the black ash swale is not tenanted by many birds and squirrels as are the ridges, and only the striped woodpecker or a wandering jay fluttered about at times, or a coon might seek the pools for frogs. Harlson had circumstance for thought. Only the hard labor cleared his blood and brain, and helped him.

Could fortune come to him who had such a load upon his conscience? Was not he a violator of all law, as he had learned it,—law of both God and man? Had he an excuse at all, and what was the degree of it? He could not endure the time when it became too dark in the wood for work, and when he drove the jaded oxen out into the field and to the barn, and it was yet too early for seeking the hay-mow, which was of clover, and there seeking sleep. A clover mow is a wonderful sleep-compeller. There are the softness and fragrance, but, sometimes, even with that, he would be wakeful. To avoid himself, the young man would, at last, go in early evening to the older farmers' homes,—for it was his own country and he knew them all,—and there, with the sons and hired men, pitch quoits in the road before the house.

Quoits is still a game of farmers' sons, and the horseshoe is superior to the quoit of commerce and the town. The open side affords facility for aggressive feats of cleverness in displacing an opponent's cast, and the corks upon the shoes reduce some sliding chances, and the game has quality. And Harlson found rather a distraction in the contests. He found, maybe, distraction, too, in chatting with slim Jenny Bierce, who was a very little girl when he was in the country school, but who had grown into almost a woman, and who was a trifle more refined, perhaps, than most of her associates. She had a sweetheart, a stalwart young farmer named Harrison Woodell, one of the schoolmates of Harlson's early youth, but she liked to talk with Harlson. He was different from her own lover; no better, of course, but he had lived another life, and could tell her many things.

And Woodell, who expected to marry her, glowered a little. She did not care for that. Grant Harlson had not noticed it.

But neither quoits nor Jenny Bierce sufficed at all times for forgetfulness. Harlson was in the grasp of that enemy—or friend—who gives vast problems, and with them no solution. He could not rest. He read his Bible, but that only puzzled him the more, because there seemed to him, of necessity, degrees of wrong, and he could not find a commandment which was flexible. He chafed because there was no measure for his sentence.

A pebble at the rivulet's head will turn the tiny current either way, and so change the course of eventual creek and river. The pebble fell near the source in Grant Harlson's case, for never before in his life had he studied much the moral problem. His had been the conventional training, which is to-day the training which asks one to accept, unreasoning, the belief of yielding predecessors, and, until he felt the prick of conscience, he had never cared to question the inheritance. Now he wanted proof. If he could not plead not guilty, might he not, at least, find weakness in the law? Then fell the pebble.

It was only a country newspaper, and it was only the chance verses clipped from some unknown source which turned the tide that might have grown yet have run forever between narrow banks.

For the verses—who wrote them?—were those of that brief poem which has made more doubters than any single revelation of the hollow-heartedness of some famed godly one; than any effort of oratory of some great agnostic; than any chapter of any book that was ever written:

I think till I'm weary of thinking, Said the sad-eyed Hindoo king, And I see but shadows around me, Illusion in every thing.

How knowest thou aught of God, Of His favor or His wrath? Can the little fish tell what the lion thinks, Or map out the eagle's path!

Can the Finite the Infinite search! Did the blind discover the stars? Is the thought that I think a thought, Or a throb of a brain in its bars?

For aught that my eyes can discern, Your God is what you think good—Yourself flashed back from the glass When the light pours on it in flood.

You preach to me to be just, And this is His realm, you say; And the good are dying with hunger, And the bad gorge every day.

You say that He loveth mercy, And the famine is not yet gone; That He hateth the shedder of blood And He slayeth us every one. You say that my soul shall live, That the spirit can never die: If He was content when I was not, Why not when I have passed by?

You say I must have a meaning: So must dung, and its meaning is flowers; What if our souls are but nurture For lives that are greater than ours?

When the fish swims out of the water, When the birds soar out of the blue, Man's thoughts may transcend man's knowledge, And your God be no reflex of you!

One night in after life I sat with Grant Harlson, in his rooms in a great city, and he told me of this, his time of doubt and tribulation, and repeated to me the poem.

"The questions it asks have not yet been answered, so far as I know," said he, "and I do not think they can be by the alleged experts in such things."

Then a sudden fancy seized him, and he broke out with a novel proposition:

"You have little to do to-morrow, nor have I much on my hands. Speaking of this to you has awakened an old interest in me and made me curious. Help me to-morrow. We'll make up now a list of twenty leading clergymen. I know most of them personally, and some of them can reason. We'll each take a cab and each visit ten, exhibiting these verses, going over them stanza by stanza, explaining the doubts they have aroused, and asking for such solution as the clergymen have, and such solace as it may afford. That will be rather an interesting experiment, will it not?"

I fell in with his whim, and the next day we made the rounds agreed upon.

What a curious thing it was! How men of various creeds felt confident and repeated the old platitudes, and would be anything but logical! How one or two were honest, and said they could not answer.

And how absurd, we said at night, the keeping of men to tell us what can no more be learned in a theological school than in a blacksmith shop, and in neither place as well as in the woods or on the sea! Yet there was no scoffing in it. We were neither irreligious.

To this young man building the fence there came a resisting mood, and he was puzzled still, but slept more pleasantly again upon his clover-mow. He was groping, but less despondent, that was all. It seemed all strange to him, for the old farm life had become largely a memory, and it was but yesterday that he was in college, one of a thousand, full of all energy and lightsomeness, and here he was alone in the wood as in a monastery, and all else was somehow like a dream. Only the oxen and the logs and the ax and the maul and the growing fence were real by day. But, in the evening, there was Jenny Bierce, and she was very real, as well as charming.

Ho wondered if she cared for him. She was apparently pleased when he found her, and they had taken long walks alone in the twilight. Once he had kissed her, and she had not been angry. What sort of drift was this, and why was he so carried by it? How different it all was from even the life of a few weeks ago! Then there came before his eyes a picture of the great, splendid animal in town, and it remained with him. It bothered him for many a day and night.

If the Hindoo king were right, if all were so undefined, why not do as did the birds and squirrels, and seek all sunny places? He could not work at his fence Sunday. He had not done that yet, but he would walk the miles Saturday night and spend his Sunday in the town.

As he thought, so he did. He did not swing the maul late the next Saturday that came, but took up his journey and reached home in early evening.

He had been absent but three weeks, yet his family had much to ask, and his father laughed at his hardened palms, and congratulated him. He changed his garb and took the way toward Mrs. Rolfston's. She had not looked for him sooner, though she knew men well, for she had seen his growing trouble and she knew his will. Her eyes blazed as might the eyes of some hungry thing to which food is brought. It was late when he reached his home again, and the next day he must read a book, he said, that he had found at Mrs. Rolfston's. At night he was stalking across the country again, to his couch on the dry clover; and he thought not even of the Hindoo king. Mrs. Rolfston's school of theology was not of the sort which worries one with puzzling things, and he had been in a receptive mood.

The next day he worked like a giant. In the early evening he found Jenny Bierce. She questioned him, but he had not much to answer.

"Is there some one in the town ?" she asked.

"There are several hundred people there."

"You know what I mean. Is there any one in particular?"—this poutingly.

He said that of late the only one, to speak of, he had found anywhere was a girl in a calico dress.

CHAPTER XI

SETTLING WITH WOODELL

So passed the days away. What added brawn came to the strong young fellow's arms from the driving of the rails and lifting them to place! Brown, almost, as the changing beech-leaves his face, and the palms of his hands became like celluloid. He was unlike the farmers, though, for he lacked the farmers' stoop—he had not to dig nor mow, nor rake nor bind. He swung his ax or maul, and commanded the red oxen in country speech, and deeper and deeper into the forest grew the fence. And, of evenings, he was with Jenny, and Sundays he was in the town. What days they were, with all their force, and health, and lawless abandonment, though in the line of nature. He drank not, nor smoked, nor ate made dishes. He was like an unreasoning bobolink, or hawk, or fawn, or wolf. But there grew apace the problem of Jenny.

One night, as the two were walking, each caught a glimpse of something dark, which moved swiftly through the bushes some distance from the road.

The girl started.

"What is the matter?" Harlson said.

"Did you not see it—that shadow in the bushes?"

"Yes. Some one was there. What of it? Some of the boys are

coon-hunting."

"It wasn't that," she whispered. "I know what it was. It was Harrison Woodell, and he is watching."

"Well, he might be in much better business. Are you fond of him?"

"I like him very much," she answered, simply, "but sometimes I am afraid."

He laughed.

"He'll not hurt you. He dare not."

"But he may hurt you."

Another laugh.

"Don't you think I can take care of myself?"

"Oh, yes"—hurriedly—"but one of you may get hurt, and I don't want anything to happen to either of you. Oh, Grant! You must be careful!"

He was impressed, though he did not show it. There may have been some of that magnetic connection, of which the scientists have told us so little, between minds tending toward each other, with sinister intent or otherwise, when all conditions are complete. Harlson felt in his heart that the girl's apprehensions were not altogether groundless, but, as was said, he was in perfect health and had a pride, and he cast away the thought and but made love. And he prospered wickedly. It was late when the girl reached her home again, and she went in tremblingly and silently. So bent had been their footsteps that neither Harrison Woodell nor other living thing could have been near them and unseen.

Down the tree-fringed roadway and across the field to the barn went Harlson, and wondered somewhat at himself. Into what had he developed, and how would it all end? He was elated, but uneasy. He was glad the fence was nearing completion, and that with the money due him life in the big city would begin. He clambered upon the clover-mow, and tossed about uneasily on the blanket upon which he had thrown himself still dressed. It was some time before he slept, and then odd dreams came.

He thought he had taken Jenny to the town, and that Mrs. Rolfston seemed always near them, yet in hiding. They could not get away from her. Then came a time when she had crept up behind them and over his head had thrown a noose, and was drawing it tighter and tighter and strangling him, and he could not, somehow, raise his hands to free himself. He was suffocating! He struggled in his agony and awoke—awoke to find his dream no dream at all! to feel a hand on his throat, a knee upon his chest, and to know that he was being choked to death!

More than once in later life Grant Harlson felt himself very near the line which men who have crossed once may not repass, but never later came to him the feeling of this moment. It was but a flash of thought, for the physical being's upheaval followed in an instant, but it was a flash of horror. Then began an awful struggle.

Borne down deeply in the yielding clover, Harlson had little chance to exert his strength, which, with that grip upon his throat, could not last long at most; but he writhed with all the force of desperation, and wrenched loose, at last, one arm, which had been pressed useless against his side. With the free hand he clutched his adversary's collar and strained at it, while he heaved with all his power to turn himself below. The couch was not far from the edge of the great mow, but of that he was not thinking, nor of the fact that the hay had, in the stowing away, been built out, so that the mow well overhung the barn floor. Well for him that it was so! There was a sudden loosening and sliding as the struggle in the darkness became fiercer, and then, parting from the mass, a section of the mow, a ton at least in weight, shot downward, carrying upon it the two men, who, as it struck the floor beneath, rolled from its surface through the great open doors, down the steep incline, up which wagons were driven on occasion, and leaped to their feet together, there in the clear moonlight.

They stood glaring at each other. Grant Harlson gasping, but himself again, as he inhaled the blessed air. Each stood at bay and watchful.

"Woodell!"

The man glared at him savagely.

"What does it mean! What were you going to do?"

"I was going to kill you."

"Then they would have hung you."

"No, they wouldn't; they would never have found you."

"Did you have a knife?"

"I didn't need one—if the cursed hay hadn't come away."

"What are you going to do now?"

"I'm going to kill you."

There was a look in the man's eyes which showed he was not jesting. Harlson thought very rapidly just then. He recognized the earnestness of it all, but his sudden terror was now gone. Here were light and air and even terms with the other. The effect of the choking had passed away. He felt himself a match for Woodell.

With the revulsion of feeling came then suddenly upon him a

rage against this would-be midnight slayer so great that he was calm in his very savagery. He laughed, as was his way.

"You were very foolish. You should have brought a knife or club. Kill me! Why, man, do you suppose if you were to try to get away now I would let you go? I want you, you murderer, I want you!" And he reached out his hands toward the other and opened and shut them clutchingly; and then with a snarl Woodell leaped forward and the two men grappled like bull-dogs.

Well for Harlson was it that through all the weeks he had been swinging the maul and ax, and that his muscles were hard and his endurance great, for Woodell was counted one of the strong men of the region. As it was, in point of sheer strength, the two were about evenly matched, but there was a difference in their resources. One was gymnasium-trained, the other not.

In country wrestling there are the side-hold, and square-hold, and back-hold, and rough-and-tumble, the last the catch-as-catch-can of stage struggles. In early boyhood Harlson had learned the tricks of these, and in the college gymnasium he had supplemented this wisdom by persistent training in every device of the professional gladiators. He was there considered something better than the common. And this, though a life depended on it, was but a wrestling-match. It was but a struggle to see which should get the other in his power, and blows count but little in a death-grapple.

They swayed and swung together, but so evenly braced and firm that minutes passed, while, from a little distance, they would have seemed but motionless. All who have watched two well-matched wrestlers will recognize this situation.

In each man's mind was a different immediate aim. Woodell wanted Harlson on the ground and underneath him; he wanted his hand upon his throat, and to clutch that throat so savagely and so long that the man's face would blacken and his tongue protrude, and his limbs finally relax, and the work attempted on the hay-mow be done completely! Harlson had but one thought: to overmaster in some way his assailant.

There was a sudden change, a mighty movement on the part of Woodell, and in an instant the struggle was over.

Glorious are your possibilities, O pretty grip and heave, O half-Nelson, beloved of wrestlers! What a leverage, what a perfection of result is with you! What a friend you are in time of peril! Woodell, too bloodthirsty to feint or dally, released his hold and stooped and shot forward, his arms low down, to get the country hold, which rarely failed when once secured. And, even as he did so, in that very half-second of time, there was a half-turn of the other's body, an arm about his neck, a wrench forward to a hip, and, big man though he was, nothing could save him!

His feet left the earth; he whirled on a pivot, high and clear, and came to the ground with a force to match his weight, his body, like a whip-lash, cracking its whole length as he struck.

Stunned by the awful shock, he did not move. His adversary stood glaring at the still form for a moment, dazed himself by the sudden outcome, then dashed into the barn, came out with a harness throat-latch and a pitchfork, strapped Woodell's hands together, pulled them over his knees, and between the knees and wrists passed the long ash fork-handle. The man, slowly recovering his senses, was "bucked" in a manner known to any schoolboy; as securely bound as if with handcuffs and with shackles; as helpless as a babe!

CHAPTER XII

INCLINATION AGAINST CONSCIENCE

The shock had affected Woodell very much as what is known as a "knock-out" in sparring affects a man. Absolutely unconscious at first, he recovered intelligence slowly, though practically uninjured. Harlson stood beside the grotesquely trussed figure and watched the return to consciousness with curiosity. The cool night air assisted the restoration.

Woodell opened his eyes, seemed to be wondering where he was, and then, as realization came, made an attempt to rise. The effort was ridiculous, and he but flopped like a winged loon. The ontortion of his face was frightful as there came upon him full understanding of his situation. He struggled fiercely once again, then lay quiet, looking up at Harlson with malignant eyes.

Harlson's fit of rage had gone entirely. There had come upon him a swift compunction. "Why did you try to murder me?" he asked.

"You know well enough,—you!" came from between the teeth of the man on the ground.

"I do not. I can't understand it! Have I ever injured you?"

"Injured me? You dodging, lying thief! What are you quibbling for? You know just how you have injured me. Why don't you finish the thing? Get a club and knock out my brains! They won't hang you, for you can say it was in self-defense, and my being here will prove it. Do it! Have a complete job of what you have done this summer!"

The man, writhed in his ignoble position, and tears gushed from his eyes. Harlson reached forward and withdrew the pitchfork handle. Woodell scrambled to his feet ungracefully, for his hands were still strapped together before him.

"Look here, Woodell," said Harlson, "let us go to the road and walk down toward your place. I'll not unstrap your hands just yet. I think I'll feel a trifle more comfortable having you as you are. I want to talk with you. I want you to be fair with me. Was it because of Jenny Bierce?"

"You know it was."

"But why haven't I as good a right to make love to Jenny as you or any other man?"

Woodell turned fiercely: "More quibbling." Then in a tone of demand: "Tell me this: Are you going to marry her?"

Harlson hesitated. "I don't know."

"You do know! You know you haven't any idea of such a thing. You are just amusing yourself until you get your cursed fence built."

"What is that to you?"

"To me! She was engaged to be married to me, and we were happy together until you came; and you've come, broken up two lives and done no one any good, not even yourself, you hungry wolf! She cares more for me to-day than she does for you. She is better suited to me! But with your trick of words and your ways you tickled her fancy at first, and, finally, you charmed her somehow as they say snakes do birds. And she'll not be fit for anybody when you go away!" The big man sobbed like a baby.

Harlson made no immediate reply. Was not what Woodell was saying but the truth? Did he really care for Jenny or she for him? What had it been but pastime? He could give her up. It would be a little hard, of course. It is always so when a man has to surrender those close relations with a woman which are so fascinating, and which come only when there has been established that sympathy between them which, if not love, is involuntarily considered by each something that way. There was a struggle in his mind between the instinct to be honorable and straight-forward and fair, and to do what was right, and the impulse, on the other hand, to refuse anything demanded by an assailant. But the would-be murderer was not a murderer, after all. He was only a temporary lunatic whom Harlson himself had driven mad. That was the just way to look at it. As for Jenny, she would not suffer much. There had not been time enough. Not in a day does a man or woman have that effect produced upon the heart which lasts forever. So, were he to disappear from the affair, nothing very serious, nothing affecting materially the whole of any life would follow. The odds were against him, or rather against the worst side of him, in the reflection.

He acted promptly. "I don't know about it," he said; "I'm puzzled. I don't care much. I don't know just where I stand, anyhow. I want to be decent, but it seems to me I have some rights; I'm all tangled up. I don't think you imagine I am afraid—I wasn't when I was a little boy in school with you as a bigger one. You know that—and I'm not now. But that doesn't count. I've been studying over a lot of things, and I don't know what to do. I think you may be right, and that I have been all wrong. I give it up. But I do know that a fellow can't make any mistake if he tries to do what is right, and, in figuring out the thing, takes the side that seems to be against him. He can fight, he can do anything better after he feels that he has done that. Hold on."

Woodell stopped, wonderingly. Harlson unbuckled the strap about the man's hands and threw it into the bushes at the roadside.

The farmer straightened himself up, reached out his arms, clutched his palms together, and looked at the other man. Harlson spoke bluntly.

"Yes, I know you want to try it again. But, as I feel now, it could only end one way. I don't mind. I only wanted to loose you before I say what I wanted to say, so that you wouldn't think I was making terms on my own account."

"Go on," said Woodell, gruffly, still stretching his arms.

"Well, it is just this. I don't think I've been doing the right thing. I am going to leave Jenny Bierce to you. She will not care much, and it will be all right in a little time. That is all. No, not quite! You tried to kill me. Maybe I would have been as big a fool, just such a crazy, jealous man as you, if things had been the other way. I don't know. But I do know this, that your coming here to-night, except that it has made me think, has nothing to do with what I have made up my mind to. Here we are in the road. I don't want to sleep uneasily in the barn. You tried to kill me. I have tried to decide on what is right, and I will do it. Now, I want it settled with you. Here I am! Do you want to fight?"

Woodell's face had been something worth seeing while Harlson was speaking. He had followed the words of his late antagonist closely. He grasped in a general way the intent expressed. There was a radiance on his rough features.

"Do you really mean that?"

"Of course I do. What should I say it for if I didn't?"

"Then it will be all right."

"But do you want to fight?"

"No, I don't. I won't say you could lick me. It was partly luck before. I won't give up that way. But you might. That doesn't matter. I'm sorry I tried to kill you. I was crazy. You would have been, in my place. And you won't have anything to do with Jenny again? Oh, Harlson!"

And the two shook hands, and Harlson went back to his bed on the clover-mow. He thought he had done a great and philosophically noble deed—remember, this was but a boy little over twenty—and he slept like a lamb. And next evening he went over to Woodell's home and said he wanted some supper, and after the meal laughed at Woodell, and said he was going off to another farm to pitch quoits until it got too dark, and the two young men walked down the road together and exchanged some confidences, and when they parted each was on good terms with the other. This was strange, following an attempted murder, but such things happen in real life. And it may be that Woodell had the worst of the bargain in that conversation.

He was better equipped for the winning of Jenny, but the troubled man with whom he had been talking had reached out blindly for aid in another direction. Not much satisfaction was the result. Woodell was of the kind who, if religious at all, believe without much reasoning, but Harlson had repeated to him the reasoning of the Hindoo skeptic. Woodell had at least intelligence enough to follow the line of thought, and, in after time, when he was a family man and deacon, the lines would recur to vex him sorely.

And Jenny did not pine away and die because she saw little more of Harlson. He met her and explained briefly that they had been doing wrong, and that he and Woodell had talked. She turned pale, then red, but said little. Of the struggle in the night Jenny never learned. She inferred, of course, that her lover had gone in a straightforward way to Harlson, and that his demands had been acceded to. She was gratified, perhaps, that she had become a person of much importance. She thought more of Woodell and less of Harlson, because of the issue of the debate, as she understood it, and, when the first pique and passion were over, became resigned enough to the outlook. She had been on the verge of sin, but she was not the only woman in the world to carry a secret. Woodell's pleadings were met with yielding, and the wedding occurred within a month. Perhaps she made a better wife because her husband did not know the truth in detail, and she felt the burden of a debt, but that is doubtful. Though fair of feature, she was not deep enough of mind to even brood. Of course, too, by this standard should be lessened the real degree of all erring. Harlson, wiser, was much the more guilty of the two and deserved some punishment, but, as an equation, it could, at least, since he was young, be said in his defense that as he was to Jenny so had Mrs. Rolfston been to him. The person who had changed things was that same fair animal of the town.

And shallow-minded legislatures will enact preposterous social laws for the regulation of the morals of boys, and imagine they have placed another paving-stone in the road to the millennium, while the Mrs. Rolfstons are having a riotous time of it.

CHAPTER XIII

FAREWELL TO THE FENCE

When the first frosts of autumn come the black ash swales are dry, and there is more life in them than in midsummer. Hickory trees grow in the swales, and the squirrels are very busy with the ripened nuts. The ruffed grouse, with broods well grown, find covert in the tops of fallen trees, or strut along decaying logs. There are certain berries which grow in the swales, and these have ripened and are sought by many birds. The leaves are turning slowly to soft colors. There is none of the blaze and glory of the ridges where the hard maples and beeches are, but there is a general brownness and dryness and vigor of scene. It is good. The fence was nearly done, and the money for its building was almost owned. The rails stretched away in a long line through the narrow lane hewed through the wood, the tree-tops meeting overhead, and a new highway was built for the squirrels, who made famous use of the fence in their many journeys. The woodpeckers patronized it much, and tested every rail for food, but only in a merely incidental way, for each woodpecker knew that every rail was green and tough, and sound and tenantless as yet. There was a general chirp and twitter and pleasant call, for all the young life of the year was out of nest and hole and hollow, and now entering upon life in earnest. It was a season for buoyant work.

The great maul, firm and heavy still, showed an indentation round its middle, where tens of thousands of impacts against the iron wedges had worn their way, and even the heads of the wedges themselves were rounded outward and downward with an iron fringe where particles of the metal had been forced from place. The huge hook at the end of the log chain was twisted all awry, though no less firm its grip. The fence, the implements and all about showed mighty work, something of mind, but more of muscle.

Most perfect of all tonics is physical, out-door labor, particularly in the forest, and it is as well for mind as body. It eliminates what may be morbid, and is healthful for a conscience. Why it is that, under most natural conditions which may exist, the conscience is not so nervously acute, is something for the theologians to decide,—they will decide anything,—but the fact remains. The out-door conscience is strong, but seldom retrospective.

Grant Harlson swung his maul and delighted in what was about him, and breathed the crisp October air, scented with the spice bushes he cut to clear the way, and pondered less and less upon the puzzles of the Hindoo king. His mood was all robust, and when he visited the town he was a wonder to Mrs. Rolfston, who was infatuated with the savagery of his wooing and madly discontent with the certainty that she must lose him. She made wild propositions, which he laughed at. She would remove to the city; she would do many things. He said only that the present was good, and that she was fair to look upon. And from her he would go to his other sweetheart, the great maul, and be faithful for six days of the seven. He did not work as late of afternoons now. He was enjoying life again in the old healthful, boyish way.

He had a friend from town with him, too—a setter, with Titian hair and big eyes, which slept on the clover beside him, and an afternoon or two a week he would take dog and gun and go where the ruffed grouse were or where a flock of wild turkeys had their haunts among the beech trees. He would announce, with much presumption and assurance, at some farm-house door, that he would be over for dinner to-morrow, and that it would be a game dinner, and that he would leave the game with them on his way back that same evening. There would be chaffings and expressions of doubt as to reliance upon such promise and "First catch your rabbit" comment, but they were not earnest words, for his ability as a mighty hunter was well known.

Craft and patience are required when the wild turkey is to be secured, for it is wise in its generation, and will carry lead, but it is worth the trouble, for no pampered gobbler of the farm-yard has meat of its rich flavor. Beech-nuts and berries make diet for a bird for kings to eat. And when Harlson brought a couple of noble young turkeys to the board the banquet was a great one, and the boys pitched quoits that night no better for it. A good thing is the wild turkey, but even a better thing, when his numbers and quality are considered, is the ruffed grouse, the partridge of the North, the pheasant of the South. How, in the lake region, he dawdles among the low-land thornberry bushes in autumn, how he knows of many things to eat beside the thorn-apples, and how plump he gets, and how cunning! How watchful he is, how knowing of covert, and with what a burst he lifts himself from his hiding-place and whirls away between the tree-trunks! How quick the eye and hand to catch him when he rises from the underbrush and is out of sight in the wood before the untrained sportsman stops him with what is little more than a snapshot, so instantaneously must all be done! Yet what a dignified thing is he, and how easy to find by one who knows his ways and what hold habit has upon his gray-brown majesty. Should the sudden shot fail, there is the fatal weakness of the bird of flying, as the bee flies, straight as an arrow goes, and of alighting high, say about two hundred yards away, and trusting to the trick which fools all other enemies to fool the man. Following the straight line of his flight, scanning the tree-tops, will you note at last, upon some great limb and close to the tree's trunk, an upright thing, slender, still-hued, silent and motionless. It is so like the wood it well might miss the tyro. It is not unsportsmanlike, it is in fair chase to shoot, and then there comes to the ground, with a great thump, the cock of the northern woods, and you have one of the prizes man gets by slaying. But this is only in the wood. In the open it is quite another thing. What a toothsome bird, too, is your ruffed grouse, how plump and yet gamey to the taste! You must know how to cook him, though. He must be broiled, split open neatly and well larded with good butter, for not so juicy even as the quail is the ruffed grouse, and he must have aid. But, broiled and buttered and seasoned, well, what a bird he is!

There were woodcock, too, in the lowlands, and Harlson found with them such buoyant life as we men find in sudden death of those small, succulent creatures. To stop a woodcock on the wing as it pitches over the willows is no simple thing, and he who does it handily is, in one respect, greater than he who ruleth a kingdom. And, at the table—but why talk of the woodcock? There are other game birds for the eating, good in their various degrees, but the woodcock is not classed with them. In him is the flavoring drawn by his long bill from the very heart of the earth, the very aroma of nature, and all richness. They ate peacocks' brains in Caesar's time. Later, they found there was something greater in the ortolan, and in some of the similar smaller things which fly. But as the ages passed, and palates became cultivated by heredity, and what made all flavors became known, the woodcock rose and was given the rank of his great heritage—the most perfect bird for him who knows of eating; the bird which is to others what the long-treasured product of some Rhine hillside or Italian vineyard is to the vintage of the day, what old Roquefort or Stilton is to curd, what the sweet, dense, musky perfume of the hyacinth is to the shallow scent of rhododendron. Even the Titian-haired setter recognized the imperial nature of the woodcock, and was all emotion about the willow-clumps.

Of course, from one point of view it is absurd, to thus depart from a simple story upon the killing or the cooking or the flavor of a bird. But I am telling of Grant Harlson and the woman he later found, and it seems to me that even such matters as these, the sport he had, and the facts and fancies he acquired, are part of the story, and have something to do with defining and making clear the forming knowingness, and character, and habits and inclinations of the man. Between him who knows old Tokay and woodcock, and the other man, there is every distinction. Harlson had learned his woodcock, but the Tokay was yet to come.

And the fence neared its end. The young man almost regretted it, eager as he had become to test his strength in the great city. Physically, it was grand for him. What thews he gained; what bands of muscle criss-crosses between and below his shoulders! What arms he had and what full cushions formed upon his chest! That was the maul. How he ate and drank and slept!

The days shortened, and the hoar frosts in the early morning made the fence look a thing in silver-work strung through the woods. Where the oxen had stepped in some soft place were now, at the beginning of the day, thin flakes of ice. Even in the depth of the clover-mow the change of temperature was manifest, and Harlson slept with a blanket close about him. The autumn had come briskly. And the last ash was felled, the oxen for the last time scrambled through the wood with the heavy logs, and for the last time ax and maul and wedge did sturdy service. One day Grant Harlson lifted the last rail into place; then climbed upon the fence, looked critically along it, and knew his work in the country was well done. He was absorbed in the material aspect of it just then. It was a good fence. Fifteen years later he strolled one afternoon, cigar in mouth, across the wheat-field where the wood had been, and inspected the fence he had built alone that summer, away back. The rails had grown gray from the effect of time and storms, and a rider was missing here and there, but the structure was a sound one generally, and still equal to all needs. It was a great fence, well built. He looked at the wasting evidence of the great ax strokes upon the rail ends, and said, as did Brakespeare, when he visited the castle of Huguemont and noted where his sword had chipped the stairway stone in former fight; "It was a gallant fray."

There was the getting of pay—the selling of a Morgan yearling colt sufficed the owner of the land for that—and the end of one part of one human being's life was reached. He went to town again and lived there a week or two. A life not held in bonds, but somehow under all control. It was curious; he could not understand it; but, even in the wood, he had out-grown Mrs. Rolfston. He was with her much. There was no let nor hindrance to their united reckless being, but all was different from the beginning. He was not selfish with her; he grew more courteous and thoughtful, yet the woman knew she could not keep him. There were stormy episodes and tender ones, threats and tears, and plottings and pleadings, and all to the same unavailing end. Your woman of thirty of this sort is a Hecla ever in eruption, but becoming sometimes, like Hecla, in the ages, ice-surrounded. She has her trials, this woman, but her trials never kill her. The rending of the earth, earthy, is never fatal. She recovers. With her, good digestion ever waits on appetite, though an occasional appetite be faulty.

And one day Grant Harlson left the town, his face turned cityward. The country boy—this later young man of the summer—was no more. To fill his place among the mass of bipeds who conduct the affairs of the world so badly and so blunderingly, was but one added to the throng of strugglers in one of men's great permanent encampments.

CHAPTER XIV

A RUGGED LOST SHEEP

The journal of Marie Bashkirtseff is a great revelation of the hopes and imaginings and sufferings of a girl just entering that period of life when woman's world begins. Many upon two continents have been affected by the depths and sadness of it, yet it is but a primer, the mere record of a kindergarten experience, in comparison with what would be the picture showing as plainly a heart of some man of the city. Did you ever read the diary, unearthed after his death, and printed in part but recently, of Ellsworth, the young Zouave colonel, who was slain in Alexandria, and avenged on the moment, at the very beginning of the great civil war? That is a diary worth the reading. There is told the story of not alone vain hopes and ungratified ambitions, but of an empty stomach and dizzy head to supplement the mental agony and make its ruthlessness complete. There were, too, the high courage which was sorely tested—and an empty stomach is a dreadful shackle—and the bulldog pertinacity which ever does things. That was a diary of real life, with little room for dreams, and much blood upon the pen.

It befell Grant Harlson to learn how helpless in the great city is the man as yet unlearned in all its heartlessness and devious ways and lack of regard for strangers, and the story of Ellsworth was very nearly his.

It was well enough at first. He had some money, and had

occupation at a pittance, intended only by the law firm with whom he was a student to serve for his car or cab-hire when on service outside the office. His privilege of studying with the firm was counted remuneration for his services, and he was, so far as this went, but in the position of other young men of his age and value under such circumstances, but, unlike others, he had relied upon the law of chance to aid him.

One hundred dollars does not last long when one is healthy and has a mighty appetite, and, that gone, two dollars and fifty cents a week, and hard work for it, is very little to live on, and Harlson found it so. Not for all the comforts of the world would he have written home for aid in the town. It seemed there was nothing for him to do. It had become mid-winter, and the winter was a cold one. Gaunt men followed the coal wagons or visited the places where charity is bunglingly dispensed by the sort of people who drift into smug officials at such agencies as naturally as some birds fly to worm-besprinkled furrows for their gleanings.

Harlson saw much of this, and knew his fate was not the worst among so many, and it aided him in his philosophy, but he had a mighty appetite. He was a great creature, of much bone and brawn, and being hungry was something he could not endure. He thought—how far back it seemed—of the farmers' dinners, and the turkey and ruffed grouse and woodcock. Woodcock! Why, his whole two dollars and fifty cents would not feed him for a single time upon that glorious bird! He looked through the fine restaurant windows, and it amused him. His own meals were taken in restaurants of a poorer class. With thirty-five cents and a fraction to live upon for a day, one does not care for game.

Harlson's dress became of the shabby genteel order. The binding upon coat and vest had begun to show that little wound which is not wide nor deep, but is past the healing, and the shininess at knees and elbows reflected the light that never was on land or sea, or, at least, ought not to be. He felt a degradation with it all, though it was with him the result of folly, not of fault, and he made a struggle for reform in his finances. He abandoned the cheap room in which he lived, and slept upon the office floor at night, the place in decent weather being moderately warm.

The individual from China and the individual from more than one other land, who comes to live with us, can exist on thirty-five cents a day and think his provender the fat of the land. But he is not a great meat-eater. The fiber of him is not our own. His style of tissue was not fixed in northern bay and fjord and English and Norman forests, and his ancestors transmitted to him a self-denying stomach. He can live in the city upon thirty-five cents a day, and clasp his hands across his abdomen and say, with the thankful, "I have dined." Not so the man of Harlson's type, and of his size. The sum of two dollars and fifty cents, the young man found, would not feed and clothe him for a week. He was a boy still, in the freshness of his appetite, yet his demands in quantity were manly, to a certainty. Six feet of maul-swinging humanity had eaten much, even in midsummer. That same six feet required more now, when the temperature was low and the system needed carbon. Perhaps he got all that was good for him; it is well to train down a little occasionally; but Harlson wandered about sometimes with a feeling of sympathy for the wolf of the forest, the hawk of the air, and the pickerel of the waters, all hungry ever and all refusing to live by bread alone.

As time passed this condition of things wore upon the man. His fancies, if not morbid, became a trifle ugly. He worked feverishly, but he chafed at his own ignorance of city ways, such that he could not increase his income. He sought manual labor which could be done at night, but failed even in this, for at that time he lacked utterly the way about him which fits the city, and persuades the man of business when there is little labor to be done. It was almost a time of panic. He would wander about the streets at night like a lost spirit. Sometimes he would meet old college friends. He had classmates in the city, some of them well-to-do and well established, and they were glad to meet him, the man who had done a little to give the class its record, and he was invited to swell dinners and to parties. He would but feign excuses, and to none of them told bluntly, as he should have done, just what his situation was, and how a trifling aid would make his future different. He was very proud, this arrogant product of the old Briton blending and the new world's new northwest, and he lacked the sense which comes with experience in the bearings of a life all novel, and so he remained silent, and, incidentally, hungry.

It was at this period of his career that Harlson was in closest sympathy with the sad-eyed Hindoo king. He was not doing anything out of the way; he was working hard, with clean ambitions, yet he was hungry. He could not understand it. No doubt an empty stomach inclines a man to much logic and the splitting of straws. There comes with an empty stomach less of grossness and more of abstract reason, and an exaltation which may be all impractical, but which is recklessly acute.

"I want to do things, I want to help others—I don't know why, but I do—I have ambitions, but I try to make them good. I am doing the best I can with the brains I have. I get up in the morning from the office floor and do my utmost all day, and try to do better when I get out, but nothing helps me! Where is the God who, it is said, at worst, helps those who help themselves.

"You say that we have a meaning; So has dung, and its meaning is flowers."

"The Hindoo king must be right. I am, we all are but like horses, or trees, or mushrooms; and it is only some sort of accident which makes each thing with life successful or unsuccessful, happy or unhappy, as the case may be."

So, at this time, Grant Harlson reasoned, blindly, yet in his heart there was something which protested against his own deductions and kept him in the path which was straightforward, and from staking all the future on the morrow. So drifted away the days, and this strong-limbed young fellow became hungrier and hungrier, and more shiny at knees and elbows, and more lapsided of foot-gear, and more thoroughly puzzled at, and disgusted with, the city world.

Sometimes the young man would resolve that in the morning he would abandon all his plans, and seek the country again, and there, where he could hold his own and more, live and die apart from all the feverishness and chances of another way of living. And he would awake and sniff in the morning air, and say to himself that he was a cur last night, and that he would stay and hold his own, and, in the end, win somehow. The bulldog strain asserted itself, and he was his own again. At night, after a fruitless day, he might become again depressed, but the morning restrung the bow. Sometimes—these were his weaker days—he would abandon all effort, and seek the free public library, and there plunge into books and find, for the passing time, forgetfulness. These were his only draughts of absolute nepenthe, for at night he dreamed of the yesterday or of the morrow, and it marred his rest. The library gave him, for the time, another world, though it had harsh suggestions. He would stop his reading to wonder how Chatterton felt when starving, or if Hood had as miserable a time of it as alleged, or if Goldsmith was jolly when, penniless, he argued his way through Europe, or if even Shakespeare went without a meal. But the library, on the whole, was a solace and a tonic. It rested him, since it made him, for a time, forget.

It was but characteristic of Harlson that, in the midst of all this test of endurance of a certain sort, he should do what deprived him of all chance of greater ease and greater vantage-ground with time expended out of the line he had established. One of his old college friends, guessing, perhaps, his real condition, came to him with an offer of what was more than a fair income, if he would teach one of the city's high-schools. The hungry fellow only laughed, and said that was not on his programme. He still went hungry and grew more shabby in appearance, and then came to him what was, perhaps, a sear upon his life—perhaps what broadened, educated, and made him wiser.

CHAPTER XV

THE STRANGE WORLD

One night Harlson, with a great appetite, as usual,—for he had not eaten since his scant breakfast,—went out to get his supper. It was not dinner, for he never, at that time, dined. He had in his pocket twenty cents. The next day he would get his usual weekly stipend. He would spend fifteen cents, he thought, upon his supper, then return to the office to sleep, and would have five cents remaining for the morning meal. That would do to buy buns with, and he would endure what stomach clamor might come until evening, when he would be a capitalist, and riot in all he could eat, even though he doubled a cheap order.

So he reasoned, as he went down the garish street, and looked right and left for some new restaurant, for he chanced to want a change. One's love for cheap restaurants is not perpetual. A mild illuminated sign over a small building attracted his attention. It had the aspect of what would be cheap, but clean.

Harlson entered the place and found what he had looked for. There was the small front room with scattered tables, the partition at the back, reaching but half way to the ceiling, with the usual curtained door, and there was no one in the room. He took a seat beside one of the tables and there waited. He had not long to wait. The curtains parted and a woman entered. The woman who came into the room was possibly thirty-five years of age. She was strong of frame, though not uncouth, and had keen, laughing gray eyes, heavy eyebrows and chestnut hair. She was a half jaunty, buxom amazon, with a brazen, comrade look about her, and was evidently the proprietress of the place. She came to where Harlson was seated and asked him what he wished to eat. The patron of this restaurant was studying the bill of fare intently. He wanted to get what was, as Sam Weller says, "werry fillin," at the price, and yet he had certain fancies. He looked up at the woman and said, bluntly:

"I have only fifteen cents to spend. What would you advise for the money?"

For the first time the eyes of the two met. Harlson was interested in the fraction of a second. In the fraction of a second he knew that it was not a restaurant pure and simple that he had entered, for he had learned much already in the city. The woman who looked at him was not merely the proprietress of a place where food was sold.

The woman did not answer at once. She was looking at the customer. She pulled out the chair opposite him and sat down.

"Have you lived here long?" she said.

Harlson had been so isolated, that to have an inquiry made in relation to his personal affairs seemed droll. It seemed something like humanity again, as well.

He studied more closely the woman opposite. She did not convey any idea of a creature of innate dishonesty or treacherous character. She had the appearance of being a shrewd, merry, healthy sinner. He forgot that she owed him an answer as he met her question:

"No, I have not lived here long, but I am as hungry as if I had lived here for half a century. What shall I order?"

She looked at him curiously. His language was not of the kind she had been accustomed to. She measured him from head to heel, while he noted her examination and was amused, and showed it in his face. She blushed, or rather flushed, and measured him again. Then she told him what he should order most wisely for the sum he had named. He was surprised at the quantity and quality of it.

The woman, meanwhile, had left him without further comment. As he was ending his meal, she came in again and took the seat in front of him.

"You are hungry," she said.

"I was, decidedly. I'm not now."

She looked him over.

"You have spent only fifteen cents. What is the matter?"

He was surprised. He looked into her eyes and was perplexed. Why should this woman ask him this question? But he could see nothing in those eyes save a gray inquisition.

"I had only that much to spend to-night, that's all. Do you see anything absurd about it?"

The woman was puzzled in turn. She looked into the man's face in a fearless way enough, but did not know what to say. Then again came that odd way of looking over him. Finally she broke out:

"You haven't any more money, and yet you put on airs. I like it."

"I am much obliged," said he.

"That isn't fair. You know what I mean. And you know already—you're not a fool—what this place is. It is mine. The little restaurant in front is but a part. Women come here—and men. Two women live here. Did you think that?"

Harlson said he had inferred, since he came in, that the restaurant was not a restaurant alone.

"It's a funny world," he said.

She was bothered. "I don't know what you mean about the world, and I don't care. But I would like to know what your business is, and how you are doing?"

"I am not doing well, and get hungry sometimes. Had it not been for that I should not have come here to-night. But what is it to you?"

"Can't you see? Why am I talking to you?"

"I don't know."

She looked at him steadily again.

"What do you want?" was his inquiry.

"Where do you live?"

"I have no bed. I am in a lawyer's office. I can't afford a boarding-house just now, and I sleep on the office floor."

"How do you like that?" she asked.

"I don't like it."

"Then why do you stay there?"

"Where else would I sleep? I have only so much a week."

"Would you like to stay here to-night?"

"Maybe. This is better than the office floor; at least I imagine it is."

The curtains parted and there was a heavy step upon the floor. A man came in. He stopped and looked at the couple grimly. He was a big man whose cheeks had jowls and whose eyes were red. He had the air of a bully. He seemed perfectly at ease and conscious of his status, and the woman started, then looked up half anxiously and half defiantly. The man spoke first:

"What are you doing here?"

"I am talking with this gentleman at the table."

"You mustn't talk with these fellows. Get out of here!" he said, turning to Harlson.

Harlson was not really in a pleasant frame of mind; he had been too hungry. It was not the occasion on which a flabby bully should have thus addressed him. He did not answer the man, but turned to the woman.

"Is that your husband?" he asked.

"No."

"What is he, then?"

It was the intruder who answered, violently:

"She belongs to me, and you'd better get out of here."

"I don't belong to him! He has lived here, but I want to get away from him! Now," turning recklessly to the man, "you may do what you please!"

The man paid little note to what the woman said. His attention was bestowed upon Harlson.

"Look here, young fellow! Get out of this, and get out quick! You're in the way!"

Now, upon this young man Harlson, during this conversation, had come a certain increased ill humor. He was in no violent mood, as yet, but he was not, as has been said, one for a big flabby brute to thus annoy. He was quiet enough, though.

"I've come into a restaurant to get my supper."

The man's red face became redder still. "If you don't get out, I'll throw you out!"

Harlson stood up. "I'll not go!" he said, and then the man rushed upon him.

It was only a clean, quick blow, but there was no check nor parry to mar its full effectiveness. The man plunged forward too confidently, the blow caught him fairly in the face, on the fullness of the cheek, just under the eye, and those bronzed knuckles cut in to the bone. It was a wicked blow, and its force was great enough to hurl the whole body back. The man whirled away under it, and he went toppling down, with his arms thrown up wildly. As he fell, he pitched still further back, in his effort to save himself, and his head struck the wainscoting as he reached the floor. Blood gushed from his cut cheek. It was a moment or two before he clambered slowly to his feet.

"Shall I hit you just once more?" was Harlson's query.

The man did not answer. The woman stood looking on curiously, but saying nothing. Harlson waited for a time, then told his assailant to go away; and the man picked up his hat and stumbled out upon the street.

The woman sat down again. It was some time before she spoke.

"You are strong, and will fight," she said.

"I had nothing else to do."

"Do you want to stay here?"

"It is better than the office floor."

"Will you stay here?"

He hesitated. It was a turning-point in his life, and he knew it. There was something rather startling to him in it.

Then came the swift reflection: He wanted to know all of life. This was the under-life, the under-current, of which reformers prate so much and know so little. Why not be greater than they? Why not have been a part of it, and in time to come speak knowingly? He was but a part of this world, as accident had made it. He hoped if the world wagged well to be a protector for certain weak ones. It was a world wherein immediate brute force told. Well, he could supply that easily enough. And what would he not learn? He would learn the city, the ignorance of which had resulted in his being hungry—he, a young man college-bred, and with some knowledge of Quintilian's crabbedness, or the equations of X and Y in this or that or the Witch of Agnesi. And were not these people part of the world, and was not this life something of which he ought to know the very heart?

Still, there were relations of things to be considered. There were people at home, and it would not do.

Then, just as he turned to refuge the woman who sat looking at him, the curtains parted again and a face appeared. It was the face of a woman, not of the world about him. It was some accident, some sinister, unexampled happening, which had brought the face to the surroundings. It gave to the wavering man a new idea of this world of shame and sin, and it may have been the deciding ounce.

CHAPTER XVI

THE REALLY UGLY DUCKLING

He turned, to the woman across the table: "All right; I will stay."

I am but telling the story of a man of whose life from this time for two years I know but little. He was always reticent about these years, yet always said he had no occasion to regret them. With the life's outlines, though, with what it really was, aside from details, I became, in a degree, familiar.

What does the average person in one class know of the life in another? There are "classes," certainly, with great bars between them here, though this is a republic, and all men and women are supposed to be free and equal and alike in most things. There are lower and wider grades of existence, such that the story of them may never be told save in patch-work or by inference, yet which have as full a history, and where there are loves and hates and hopes and despairs as deep as are ever felt in the mass where the creed-teachers and Mrs. Grundy and the legislatures are greater factors.

And of this more reckless, hopeless people Harlson learned much. With them he was; of them he could never fully be. The extent to which a man is permanently defiled by pitch-touching cannot, of course, be known. It depends upon the pitch and upon the man. It was not a quiet life the young man led! On the contrary, it was a very feverish one, for he labored hard in the office by day—he never for an instant abandoned his ambitions and his plans—and at night he drifted into the land where were warmth and light and lawlessness. He had his duty there, such as it might be, for he was both a gambler and a protector, and, young as he was, callow as he was, within a year he had become one in demand, no trifler at the table, and an object of rivalry among those whose regard means fee of body and of soul. He, himself, at that time, did not appreciate the remarkable nature of his changing. So rapidly he aged in knowledge of all undercurrents that he passed into full maturity without a comprehension of the change. It is said that some Indians teach their children to swim, not by repeated gentle lessons, but by throwing them into a deep stream recklessly, saving them only at the last moment. So had some power hurled Grant Harlson into the black waters, and he had not drowned, and had taken rank among strong swimmers.

It is, as I have said, difficult to write intelligently of this portion of this man's life. I want to do him justice, for I have always cared for him; yet, from the conventional point of view, at least, nothing can excuse his lapse at this one time. He should have continued starving, I suppose, as have so many others, and have either died or won, as they did, instead of tasting all that is denied, and gaining much knowledge of the world, of much use in the future, all at the expense, perhaps, of that purity attaching to certain ignorances, as much in the man as the woman, since between the sexes all things are relative.

There were enough odd things in this most odd career. There were friendships and feuds with those who were of the lower multitude morally, but who were politicians and had their followings. There were romances of the order which makes the story of Dumas such a success upon the stage, and risks and escapes enough to satisfy the hungriest of romance-readers. It was all grotesque in its grim reality, and the young man did not know it. He was an unconscious desperado, and the odd thing about it all was the ease with which he led the double life.

In the morning, clear-headed and competent—for he did not drink at all of liquors—he appeared and was resolute at his work. He was becoming more and more considered. That he, somehow, knew the town so well, was in his favor. More than one case of importance was decided in another way from which it might have been, because of his knowledge of the outcasts and their connections, and how they had been used or trifled with on this occasion or on that one. He was zealous and studied furiously, and in the mere letter of the law became most confident. His examination was a trifling thing, and, once admitted to the bar, he did not remit his efforts. He was valuable to the firm. He was their watch-dog, and he suggested many things.

One day the senior partner called Harlson in, and a long conference was held. The younger man was offered a partnership on condition that he would make a specialty of certain branches of the firm's varied practice; but the offer had its disadvantages. It was not in the line political at all, but in one with vexatious business demands and requisites; yet it was accepted in a moment. And within the next week all the wicked, nervous night-life was abandoned, all the friendships formed there put upon probation, all the soiled sentiment made a thing to be ended surely and forgotten, if possible.

There were some wrenches to it all. Camille learns to love sometimes, and Oakhurst, the gambler, does not want to part with one who has stood a friend in an emergency. But Camille knows that, for her, few flowers are even annual, and Oakhurst is practical and a fatalist.

From that day, all his life, Grant Harlson kept away from close touch with this ever-existing group who live from day to day because they have been branded and do not care. Good friends he ever had among them, but they never claimed him, though, on many occasions, the men served him. They recognized the fact that he had never been more than an adopted wanderer among them, and rather prided themselves upon him. In later times he would occasionally exchange a word or two on that old life with some one who had grown outwardly respectable, with some one-time thug, later saloon-keeper and alderman and what may follow, and would be reminded of what happened on the night when the mirrors were all broken, and the Washington woman shot the man she was seeking, or when "we did the Coulson gang;" but it had long grown to seem unreal and dreamlike. He grew away from the memory, and there was no glamour to him in what might attract some other men to evil-doing, because to him there could be no novelty. He was a past-master in the ceremonials of fallen, reckless human nature, and the ritual bored him. He deserved no credit further than that. True, he was but young when he learned the rites, but that he was not still a member of the order was only because his ambition was dominant and his tastes had changed. That his will was strong, that he had tastes to develop, was because of the blood which filled his veins, and of nothing else. He had gone with a current absolutely, though swimming and always keeping his head above water until he swam ashore. Yet, as told in the beginning of this chapter, he always said to me that he did not regret this experience of abandonment. And he became a man seeking place and money.

He liked to visit his old home, and was faithful to his old crony, his aging mother, still; and, for a time, after any of these sojourns among the birds and squirrels and in the forest, he would be distrait and preoccupied with something; but all this would wear off, and then would come the press for place and pelf again. He was not entirely unsuccessful, and finally he married, as a prospering young man should—married a woman with money and presence for a hostess, and with traits to make her potent. He lived with her for a season, and found another, without his dreams and sympathies and understandings, but with a will and a way.

I do not care to tell the story of it,—indeed, I do not know it,—but the man learned the old-fashioned lesson, which seems to hold good still, that for a really comfortable wedded life a little love, as a preliminary, is a good thing always—

usually a requisite. The woman lacked neither perception nor good sense. It was she who proposed, since they were ill-mated, they should live apart, and he consented, with only such show of courtesy as might conceal his height of gladness. There were money features to the arrangement made, and it was all dignified and thoughtful. The world knew nothing of the agreement, though that generation of vipers, the relations of Mrs. Grundy, wondered why Mr. Harlson's wife and he so lived apart, and if either of them were opium-eaters, or dangerous in insane moods. The relations of Mrs. Grundy have the reputation of the universe on their hands, and, the task being one so great, they must be pardoned if they err occasionally.

From the day he was alone, Grant Harlson appeared himself again, and I speak knowingly, for I was with him then. His old self seemed then restored. The buoyancy of boyhood was his as it had never been to me since we were young together. It matters not what a chance,—this is a land where all men drift about,—but I was in the city near him now, and the old relationship was resumed. We rioted in the past of the country, and we visited it together. As time went on, Harlson seemed to forget that he was, or ever had been, a married man, and eventually the woman found other things in life than awaiting old age without social potency, and suggested, from a distance, that the separation be completed. Perhaps there was another man. I know that Harlson did not hesitate. He responded carelessly, and then reverted to things practical.

The reflection came that the mismated in this present age must ordinarily bear the burden to the end. Collusion, which in such case is but a term for a mutual business agreement, is not allowable. The social problem is a puzzle the solution of which is left to those whose ideas were given to them stereotyped. The separation was delayed, but was, vaguely, a thing possible. And Harlson laughed and threw out his arms, and made friends of many women.

They were the variety of his life, which else was a hard-working one. He was not a saint nor a deliberate sinner. He but drifted again.

CHAPTER XVII

"EH, BUT SHE'S WINSOME"

"Eh, but she's winsome!"

Grant Harlson entered my room one evening with this irrelevant exclamation.

I have remained unmarried, and have learned how to live, as a man may, after a fashion, who has no aid from that sex which alone knows how to make a home.

Harlson, at this time, had apartments very near me, and we invaded each other's rooms at will, and were a mutual comfort to each other, and a help—at least I know that he was all this to me. I have never yet seen a man so strong and self-reliant or secretive—save some few who were misers or recluses, and not of the real world—who, if there were no woman for him, would not tell things to some one man. We two knew each other, and counted on each other, and while I could not do as much for him as he for me, I could try as hard. He knew that.

"Eh, but she's winsome!"

He went to the mantel, took a cigar, and lit it, and turned to me indignantly:

"You smoke-producing dolt, why are you silent? Didn't you hear my earnest comment? Where is the trace of good behavior you once owned?"

"Who's winsome?"

"She, I tell you! She—the girl I met to-night. And you sit there and inhale the fumes of a weed, and are no more stirred by my announcement than the belching chimney of an exposition by the fair display around it!"

"You big, driveling idiot, how can I know what you are talking about? You come in with an obscure outburst of enthusiasm over something,—a woman, I infer,—and because the particular tone, and direction, and mood of your insanity is not recognized within a moment, you descend to personalities. If your distemper has left you reason enough for the comprehension of words, sit down and tell me about it. Who's winsome? What's winsome? And have you been to a banquet?"

"There is a degree of reason in what you say—that is, from the point of a clod. I'll tell you. I've met a woman."

"I dare say. There are a number in town, I understand."

"Spoken in the vein of your dullness. A person not sodden with nicotine and dreams would have recognized the fact that I had met a Woman, one deserving a large W whenever her name is spelled, a woman of the sort to make one think that all poems are not trickery, and all romances not romance."

"What's her name?"

"Do you suppose I'll tell you, you scheming wife-hunter! If I do, you'll get an introduction somehow, and then you'll win her, for I'm afraid she has good sense."

And Harlson laughed and looked down in the brotherly way he had.

"But this is nonsense. Why don't you tell me something about her? Is she fat and fifty and rich, or bread-and-buttery and white-skinned and promising, or twenty and just generally fair to look upon, or twenty-five and piquant and knowing, or some big, red-haired lioness, or some yellow-haired, blue-eyed innocent, with good digestion and premature maternal ways, or—"

"Rot! She's a woman, I tell you!"

"All right. Answer questions now categorically."

"Go ahead."

"How old is she?"

"Twenty-seven or eight."

"Married?"

"No."

"Ever been married?"

"Certainly not."

"How do you know?"

Harlson looked surprised, and then he became indignant again.

"Alf," said he, "you have good traits, but you have paralysis of a certain section of your brain. You don't remember things. Don't you think I could tell whether or not a woman were married?"

I did not answer him off-hand. I could not very well. He knew that his reply had set me thinking of many a curious test and many a curious experience. Harlson had an odd fad over which we had many a debate.

It occurred usually upon the street cars. He would make a study of the women in the car when we were together—it seemed to amuse him—and tell me whether they were married or not. He would not look at their hands—that would be a point of honor between us—but only at their eyes, and then he would say whether any particular woman were married or single, and we would leave it to the rings to decide.

Sometimes he would lose, but then he would only say: "Well, if she didn't wear a wedding ring she should have done so," and would pay for the cigars we smoked.

He had some sort of fancy about their eyes which I could never quite understand. He said that a woman who had been very close to a man, who had been part of him in any way, had nevermore the same look, and that the difference was perceptible to one who knew the thing. I tested him more than once, and I found that he had never actually failed. Sometimes the woman with the look had proved unmarried, but there were facts that made the difference.

One night Harlson and I were wandering about the city, mere driftwood, after a dinner, and our mood carried us into the haunts of those without the pale, not that we cared for any new emotion or excitement, but that we wanted to look at something outside the commonplace. To me there might be, of course, some novelty in the things that might confront us, though to Harlson they were, at their utmost, but a reminiscence. We went where a man alone was not in safe companionship, but there were enough who knew my companion well, and all was curious to me, without even the spice of care for self.

It chanced that at one period of the wandering, very late at night, or, rather, early morning, Harlson became hungry, and insisted upon entrance to a restaurant where were gathered the very refuse of the reckless and non-law-abiding, and I went with him, perforce, and saw a motley gathering. There were all sorts of people there, from thief to pander, all save those who might retain a claim to faint respectability. Harlson demanded comparative cleanliness at our table, and the food was fairly decent. We ate, then smoked, and looked about us.

I have seen many people, and many strange faces, but never such a person nor such a face as of an old woman who sat at that early hour of the morning at a table near us. The figure was a warped and withered caricature, the face that of a hag, a creature vixenish and viperish, and mean and crafty. It was the face of a procuress of the lowest and most desperate type, of a deformed she-wolf of the slums, of the worst there is in all abandoned human nature, and Harlson was as interested as I was disgusted and repelled. He noted the woman closely.

"By Jove! look there!" he said.

"What is it?"

"Look at her hand."

I looked. I saw a hand which was a claw, a strong, shriveled thing with long, dirty nails and a vulturous suggestion. It was not a pleasant sight. On the third finger of the left hand, though, was a slight gleam amid the carnivorous dullness. There was a slender band of gold there, a ring worn down to narrowness and thinness. I turned to Harlson, but he spoke first:

"Do you see that old wedding ring?"

"Yes."

"It's queer. It's good, too. There's a streak of what was good left in everything, it seems to me. I'm going to talk to her."

"Don't do it. She'll throw the plate in your face."

"No, she won't." And he rose and went over to the table of the beldame and sat down beside her. She looked up at him glaringly. He did not smile, nor, apparently, make any apology or excuse, but began talking to her, looking at the ring, and saying I know not what. And I watched that miserable old woman's face and wondered. There was more than one emotion shown—fierce resentment at first, then the half fear of the hound or the hound-bitch yielding to the master, and then the yielding of the heart, not touched, perhaps, for a quarter of a century. Harlson talked. The woman did not speak for minutes, then made some short reply, and then, a little later, there were tears in her old foxy eyes.

He rose, glared at the one or two hard-faced waiters who had ventured near him, and took upon a card something she said. Then he came back to me as the old woman left the place.

"Queer-looking, wasn't she?" he said.

"Decidedly," said I. "What were you talking about?"

"Oh, nothing but the ring. It's wonderful how they always wear the ring when they have the right to."

"But what was the use of it all? What came of your talk?"

"Nothing to speak of. It was only a fad of mine. I have a right to an occasional whim, haven't I? I'll be hanged if I'll see a wedding ring worn that way buried in unbought ground. The old hag was a marvel of all that is unwomanly and sinful. But that ring shall be properly buried, and the hand that wears it, because it *does* wear it. So I'm going to take the woman out of this and put her where she will not have to be a monster in order to live."

And he did what he said he would do. He found a place in some old women's home for that aged demon, and one day he made me go with him to see her. Maybe it was the different dress and the different surroundings, but, it seemed to me, her eyes were not as they were in the low restaurant. The hand that wore the thin gold ring was clean in its pitiful shrunkenness.

Stanley Waterloo

The creature looked neither hunted nor hunting. She was but an old woman going to the grave so near her, and going, I could not but imagine, to find the one who had given her that gold circlet some half century ago. I rather fancied Harlson's fad. As for him, when I told him so, he only said:

"Oh, of course. Peter told the third assistant bookkeeper to credit Harlson with such or such an amount." And he added; "If those people don't take good care of that old woman there'll be a new superintendent." But they took good care of her.

This is lugging in an incident at great length as an illustration, but I know of no other way to explain how Harlson so expressed himself when I asked him how he knew whether the woman of whom he had been talking was married or not. He felt confident enough.

"Well, what is she like? Can't you describe her? Has she seared your eyes with her loveliness?"

"She hasn't seared my eyes. She has only opened them. Listen to me, you thing of mud! She is just a little brown streak."

"That's an odd description of a woman."

"It's the correct one, though. She's just a little brown streak of a thing."

"Well, I've heard of a man in love with a dream, and in love with a shadow, but never before did I hear of one infatuated with a streak. Where did you meet this creature? Have you known her long?"

"Only for a month or so, and but slightly. We have not met half a dozen times. It was only tonight, you see, that I began to know her well. We talked together, and I got a glimpse of her real self—of her slender little body, of her earthly tenement, of course, I had an idea before. She is a lissom thing, with eyes like wells, and with a way to her which conveys the idea of wisdom without wickedness, and which makes a man wish he were not what he is, and were more fitted to associate with her."

"That's one good effect, anyhow. I don't know of any man who more needed to meet such a woman. How long do you expect this influence to last?"

"Longer than one of your good resolutions, my son; as long as she will have anything to do with me."

"Does this brown streak of a saint live in the city? Is her shrine easy of access? What are you going to do about it?"

"She's not a saint; she's a piquant, cultivated woman; but she is different, somehow, from any other I've ever met."

"You've met a good many, my boy."

His face fell a little.

"Yes," he said, "and I almost wish it were different; but the past is not all there is of being. There's a heap of comfort in that."

"Cupid has thumped you with his bird-bolt, certainly. Why, man, you don't mean to say that you're in earnest—that you are really stricken; that this promises to be something unlike all other heart or head troubles with you?"

He laughed.

"I am inclined to believe that the gravest diagnosis is the correct one."

"But how about the present Mrs. Harlson?"

No friend less close than I could have asked such a question. I almost repented it myself, when I noted the look which came upon the man's face after its utterance.

I suppose such a look might come to one in prison, who, in the midst of some pleasant fancy, has forgotten his surroundings, and is awakened to reason and suddenly to a perception again of the grim walls about him, and of his helplessness and, maybe, hopelessness. Harlson left the mantel against which he bad been leaning, and walked about the room for a moment or two before speaking.

"It's true," he said, "I am certainly a married man. The law allows it, and the court awards it, as things are in this society, bound by the tapes of Justice Shallow and the rest. I entered into a contract which was a mistake on the part of two people. They discovered their error, and rectified it as far as they could. Had they been two men or two women who had gone into ordinary business together, and subsequently discovered they were not fitted for a partnership, the law would have assisted cheerfully in their absolute separation. But with this, the gravest of all contracts, the one most affecting human welfare, no such kindness of the statutes may exist. Some of the churches say the contract is a sacrament, though the shepherd kings, whose story is our Bible, had no such thought, nor was it taught by the lowly Nazarene; but the law supports the legend, within certain limits. What are we going to do about it?"

I told him that I didn't know, and there were several thousand people—good people—in the city facing the same conundrum.

I called attention to the fact that the conventional band was a strong one at this time, and could not be burst without a penalty, even by the shrewdest. The dwarfs were so many that, united, they were stronger than any Gulliver. And I added that, in my opinion, as a mere layman, he was very well off; that he had been at least relieved of the great, continued trouble which follows a mismating, and that it would be time enough for him to chafe at the light chain still restraining him, when he was sure he wanted to replace it by another.

"It's not your fashion," I said, "to fret over the morrow, and it is my personal and profound conviction that you have no more real idea of marrying again than you have of volunteering in the service of the Akhoond of Swat—if there be an Akhoond of Swat at present. You're only wandering mentally to-night, my boy, dreaming, because this wisp of a young woman of whom you have been telling has turned your brain for the time. You'll be wiser in the morning."

All this I said with much lofty arrogance, and a great assumption of knowing all, and of being a competent adviser of a friend in trouble, but, at heart, I knew that, in Harlson's place, I should not have shown any particular degree of self-control. I have never felt the thing, but it must be grinding to occupy a position like that of this man I was addressing. The serving out of a society sentence must be a test of grit.

We dropped the discussion of the problem, and Harlson referred to it again but incidentally.

"The fact is," said he, "I had almost forgotten that I was not as free as other men. I have not regulated my course by my real condition. I've drifted, and there have been happenings, as you know well. There's Mrs. Gorse. I've never concealed anything. Those who know me at all well know my relationships, but I imagine that I have been deceiving myself. I am not a free agent—though I will be. It's not right as it is."

"And when am I to see this woman who has interested you, and restored the old colors to the rainbow? You will allow me to admire her, I suppose, if only from a distance?"

"Oh, yes! Come with me to the Laffins' to-morrow night. She'll be there, I learned, and I said I was going to be there too. Come with me. Of course, you understand that if she smiles on you at all, or if you appear to have produced a favorable impression upon her, I shall assassinate you on our way home."

I told him that I thought my general appearance and style of conversation would preserve me from the danger, and that I would take the risk and accompany him.

The next night I met Jean Cornish. We were destined to become very well acquainted.

CHAPTER XVIII

THE WOMAN

Only a little brown woman she.
Man of the world and profligate he,
Hard and conscienceless, cynical, yet,
Somehow, when he and the woman met,
He learned what other there is in life
Than passion-feeding and careless strife.
There came resolve and a sense of shame,
For she made as his motto but "Faith and fame."

The world is foolish: we cover truth;
We're barred by the gates that we built in youth.
Two were they surely, and two might stay,
But she turned him into the better way;
His thoughts were purified even when
He chafed and raged at the might-have-been;
He learned that living is not a whim,
For the soul in her entered into him.

He fights, as others, to win or fall,
And the spell of the Woman is over all.
Bravely they battle in their degree,
For—"The woman I love shall be proud of me!"
And the man and woman, the one in heart,
May be buried together or hurled apart,
But the strong will battle in his degree,
For—"The woman I love shall be proud of me!"

There were men and women, and music and flowers, and some of the people had intelligence, and I drifted about at the Laffins' party, and rather enjoyed myself. Of course I wanted to see the woman a fancy for whom had gripped Harlson so hardly. I had forgotten about her until, with a pleasant and clever person upon my arm, I had found something to eat and had come upstairs again, and released her to another. I wandered into an adjacent room, and there ran upon Harlson among a group. I was presented to Miss Cornish.

I do not know how to describe a woman. This one, whom I have known better than any other woman in the world, is most difficult of all for me to picture. She stood there, not uninterested altogether, for, no doubt, Harlson had been telling her already of his closest friend, his lieutenant in many things, and I had an opportunity to study her with all closeness as we exchanged the commonplaces. I understood, when I saw her, how it was that he had referred to her so absurdly as a little brown streak of a thing. Little she was, assuredly, and brown, and so slender, that his simile was not bad, but the brownness and the slenderness were by no means all there was noticeable of her. She was not imposing, this woman, but she was not commonplace. Supple of figure she was, and there were the big eyes this stricken friend of mine had told me of, and rather pronounced eyebrows, and her lips were full and red, and there was that fullness of the chin, or, rather, the vague dream or hint or vision of a daintily double chin at fifty, which means so much, but the forehead was what a woman's should be, and the glance of the eyes was clean and pure, though, in a clever woman's way, observant and comprehensive. It was a cultivated and fascinating woman whom I met.

We talked together, and Grant Harlson looked on gratified, and she seemed to like me. She made me feel, in her own way, that she liked me because she knew of me, and as we were talking I felt that she was paying, unconsciously, the greatest compliment she could to the man beside us. I knew it was because of the other, and of something that he had said of me, that she was so readily on terms of comradeship. And I knew, in the same connection, and from the same reasoning, that she had already begun to care as much for him as he for her—the man who, the night before, had so comported himself with me. Of course, it appears absurd that I could reach such a conclusion upon so little basis, but to tell when people are interested in each other is not difficult sometimes, even for so dull a man as I.

"You have known Mr. Harlson many years, I believe," she said, and added smilingly: "What kind of a man is he?"

"A very bad man," I replied, gravely.

She turned to him in a charming, judicial way:

"If your friends so describe you, Mr. Harlson, what must your enemies say? And what have you to say in your own defense? What you yourself have owned to me in the past is recognition of the soundness of the authority."

"I haven't a word to say. Of course, I had not expected this unfriendly villain to be what he has proved himself, but what he says is, no doubt, true. I'm going to reform, though. In fact, I've already begun."

"When was the revolution inaugurated?"

He looked at her so earnestly that there came a faint flush to her cheek. "Since my eyes were opened, and I saw the light," he answered.

She diverted the conversation by turning to me, and saying that, while the information I had given her was no doubt valuable, and that she should regulate her course accordingly, and advise all her friends to do the same, yet she felt it her duty to reprimand me for telling the truth so bluntly. She knew that I had done it for the best, but if there were really any hope for this wicked man, if he had really decided upon a new life, we ought to encourage him. Did I think him in earnest?

I told her that it hurt me to say it, but that I had no great confidence in Mr. Harlson's protestations. He was of the earth, earthy. A friend, it was true, should bear a friend's infirmities, but he should not ask other people to bear them, nor should he testify to anything but the truth. Mr. Harlson might or might not be in earnest in what he had declared, but, even if in earnest, there was the matter of persistency. I doubted seriously his ability to overcome the habits of a lifetime.

She was becoming really interested in the chaffing.

"What is the nature of Mr. Harlson's great iniquity?"

"There, Miss Cornish, I am justified in drawing the line in my reply. I have conscientiously explained that he was, in a general way, a villain of the deepest dye, but to make specifications would be unfriendly, and I know you wouldn't have me that."

Harlson said that he was very much obliged for my toleration, or would be until he got me alone, and Miss Cornish showed a proper spirit, and so I left them. But I had no evidence that she believed what I had said.

As we walked home together in the early morning, Harlson told me more of the young lady. She was living with an aunt, he said, and was, otherwise, alone in the world. She had but a little income, barely enough to live on, but she had courage unlimited, and tact, and was not insignificant as a social factor. She had the sturdiness of her ancestry, in which the name of Jean ran.

"I like it," Harlson said; "it fits her—'Jean Cornish'—little brown 'Jean Cornish'—little leopardess, little, wise, good woman."

I told him that he was mixing his similes, and that in a broad, comprehensive way he had become a fool.

"I tell you I'm in love with her already," he blurted out, "and somehow, some day, I will have her, and wear her and care for her!"

"But, my dear boy, don't be insane. There is the problem we were discussing last night. Have you a solution of it? And first catch your hare. Have you caught your pretty hare yet? I'll admit it's possible. Women are fools over such fellows as you when they should be adhesive to good, plodding members of society, like the friend who is now advising you, but Miss Cornish is not a fool, you see, and I don't think you deserve her."

"For that matter, neither do I," he answered; "but I will deserve her yet. I must do more of many things, and cease to do many things. I believe I comprehend better now than I ever did the words in the service, 'We have done those things and left undone,' and all that. But you'll see a difference. I'll make her proud of me. That's the right way to become clean, isn't it, old man?"

I said I thought it a wholesome and commendable resolution, on general principles, and, of course, the idol would gradually disintegrate. All idols were of clay. But it didn't matter about the idol, so long as the effect was produced. He might count on me any time for good advice. He only glared at me, and called me hard names, and we dropped in at the club and finished our cigars, and separated.

CHAPTER XIX

PURGATORY

And Grant Harlson made love to Jean Cornish and won her heart.

But all the time, unconsciously, he was a man of false pretensions, one dishonorable and unworthy of her. His friends knew of his marriage and its sequel. He had never concealed nor thought of concealing his condition, and it never occurred to him that Jean Cornish was not aware of it. He had supposed her, if she cared for him as he hoped, to be somewhat troubled, but to understand that he would do no mean thing, and that all would be well in time. Then came the sorrow of it, for Jean Cornish learned, quite accidentally, that Grant Harlson was a man with a living wife.

She would not believe it at first, and, when convinced, was dazed and could not understand. No such shock had ever before come into her life. This man, of whom she had made a hero, a trickster and a liar! It seemed as if the world were gone! There was a meeting and an explanation, and she learned how wrong she had been, in one way.

He put the case earnestly and desperately. He would not yield her. He knew she loved him, and he knew she was too good and wise to suffer forever herself or let him suffer because, in society, there wer blunders. There was a way out—a clean, right way—and they must take it. He could get a divorce on grounds of mere desertion, and three people, at least, would be better off. It was pitiful, the scene, one afternoon. He had called to see her, and was pleading with her. It was in the drawing-room, and there were stained windows they both remembered in later years. He had talked of his bondage and of his hopes. She was not quite herself; she was suffering too much. I know what happened. Grant told me once of the wrench of him then, and of all the scene. There had been a fierce appeal from him. He had become almost enraged.

"And so," he said, "you would have a man's marriage like the black biretta of Spain that is drawn over the prisoner's head before they garrote him?"

She did not move nor speak, but stood straight and silent, her hands hanging at her sides with the palms loosely open, the very abandonment of pathetic helplessness.

Such a little woman, to withstand a storm of passion!

As he wondered at her curiously blended strength and weakness, a sun-shaft blazed through the crimson glass of the upper window. The reddened light, falling on her up-springing almost coppery locks, seemed to the man's excited fancy a crown, of thorns, crimsoned with blood, and there was, oddly enough, a cross in the window.

The thought of another vicarious sacrifice awed him. Must this be one, too?

"Mistakes, dear, are not crimes. Can you not understand? I have been mistaken, have suffered, have atoned for my error. Is that enough?"

"But," she said, and her voice seemed to have suddenly grown old and thin, "you have no right to talk of mistakes. She is your wife."

"The biretta, that ends all, again! No, not so. It is as insane and inhuman to force two people to remain in wedlock after it has become odious to them, as it would be to force them into that marriage at first. Oh, my tender-hearted little one, can you not see that the bondage is more humiliating, more craven than is the idea of the veriest chattel mortgage? Yet you refuse to let the injured one go free, as you would not refuse the poorest prodigal whose one chance for home and happiness was passing from his sight."

"I cannot answer you when you discuss learnedly on such questions," she said, with a weary dignity, "for I have never thought about them. Why should I? It has always seemed to me that a man with more than one wife was a—a—Mormon. It is all so dreadful. Surely, if a marriage is anything, it is a vow before God."

"It is you that make the mistake now," he said, "for the mere form of marriage is nothing but the outward evidence of a union that has already taken place. The first is the vow before God—not the latter. I understand why you think all this; clergymen have so long been called upon to officiate at marriage rites that, with the fatherly assumption notable in the order all the world over, they have grown to regard themselves as the especial and heaven-appointed guardians of the institution. It is all so grotesque when one remembers how ready they are to 'solemnize'—save the mark!—marriage, no matter what the conditions. Have the candidates to be known as right and fitting persons? Is there even the simplest formula of preparatory examination? None! Two wholly unsuited people may rush into marriage—and misery—any day by simply presenting themselves before a sleek-faced person who mumbles drowsily over their clasped hands, and calls it a vow before God!—as he hurries back to his dinner!"

Still she was silent.

An errand boy trudging by whistled a few bars of the wedding march, doubtless heard that day at some open church door.

"Dear, there is a higher, holier law of the great Power, who made us what we are, than this one of slavish obedience to a tradition. Why must our feet go in the burning ruts?"

"It is not the well-worn ruts that burn, but the by-paths," she answered, "and oh! *how* they burn!"

"Let me lift you in my arms and carry you over them, then, that your feet may not touch. Do not be unjust to yourself. Cannot you see how right, how good it is? It is not as if I came to you from another woman—"

The girl faced around on him almost fiercely.

"No, you could not be so bad as that! To have felt the morning kiss of another woman, to have watched her good-night smile, and then to have come to me—that would have been too base, too degrading—I should have hated you because I despised you. I should have loathed you instead—"

"Of loving me! Be honest and true, little Jean—you do care."

"Yes, I have cared."

"And do still?"

"Yes."

Her tone was as cold and as clear as the sound of an icicle striking the frozen earth in the fall. It angered him, and his voice shook roughly.

"A man who binds up his life in the love of a woman is a fool! Because she is all the world to him, all he works to receive praise from, all he fears in the blaming, he thinks her capable of as much love as himself. And even as he watches, he sees her pass from fervor into apathy. Her affection is but the dry husks of what he hoped to find. You never cared!"

"Grant," she said, earnestly, "you have told me to be honest. I will be. I think"—with a little laugh—"that if I had been a man I should not have been a coward. I shall not be now. You wrong me and yourself when you say that I never cared. It is because my caring has been so much a part of myself that I have never been able to stand aloof and look and comment upon it. It was just me. When I lived, it lived; when I die—"

"My love!"

"When—no. I do not believe it can die even then! I think it is a part of my soul, and will outstand all time."

She hesitated as if devising words to express herself with even more sweet abandon. There was a certain loving recklessness in what she uttered now:

"Not care? I wish you, too, would understand! Perhaps it is because we care in such different ways. I don't know, but to me it has been all! There is no joy, no pleasure, however petty, through all the day, but it brings with it the swift desire to share it with you. Every morning I waken with your half-uttered name on my lips, as though, when I slipped hack through the portals of consciousness into the world of reality, I came only to find you, as a timid child awakes and calls feebly for its mother. Once, not long ago, in a street accident, such as you know of in our busy city, I seemed very close to death, and in an instant my spirit seemed to have overleaped the peril and the terrible scene, and was with you. Afterward, one who sat near me said that, while some screamed or prayed, I said only 'Grant,' and he asked, lightly, now that danger was over: 'Is the great general your patron saint?' And I—I did not know that I had said it, since the name can never be as near to my lips as it is to my heart."

Harlson did not reply. He could not then. His head was bent.

"And when you were ill—ah! then it was the hardest of all! I dreamed of the little things I could do for you—how your dear head could rest on my shoulders, and it might help to ease the pain; how I could save you from annoyances; how I could— love you!"

"Then come, love of me; I need you—we need each other."

"No, I think a woman who loves a man could scarcely bear that he had ever been bound to another still living, or even dead."

"But—"

"No. It is not right."

It is not always that even he who is right and strong in the consciousness of it, and resolute toward the end he is seeking may express himself as he would in protest against the object yielding to what is in the social world, though it be wrong. Grant Harlson looked down upon the slender figure and into the earnest face and was helpless for the time. Yet he was fixed of mind.

He was very tender with her, but this was not a man to give up easily what was his. He pleaded with her further, but in vain. She would not yield.

And so the weeks passed, with the problem yet unsolved. They were still much together, for she could not turn him away, and he would not stay away. There was more pleading on his part, and more anger sometimes. It seemed to him absurd that lives should be blighted because of a legend.

And she was unhappy, and, it may be, gradually attaining to broader views and moral bravery. Jean Cornish was courageous, but there was the legend.

And suddenly all was changed, the problem finding a solution not expected. Grant Harlson's wife was, as has been said, a woman of reason and of force, and she had her own life, with its objects. She chafed under the bond which still connected her with Harlson, and she broke it cleanly. It was she, not he, who sought divorce, and the simple logical ground of incompatibility of temperament was all that was required, in the State where she resided. There was no defense. Grant Harlson became free, and Jean Cornish, since his freedom came in this way, promised, at last, to become his wife.

CHAPTER XX

TWO FOOLS

They loved. They were to marry, but there were the conventionalities to be observed, and they could not be wed at once. That was understood by Grant Harlson, though he chafed at it a little.

There were certain months to be passed before the two would be as one completely, and those months were very sweet months to the twain. They were much together, this man and woman who were plighted to each other, for why should they not be, since they were to become man and wife, and since neither was so happy under other circumstances? They were not what a profound, unsentimental person would consider models of common-sense, but they were not depending upon the opinions of profound, unsentimental persons for anything in particular; so this did not affect them.

They exhibited no great interest in society, though each commanded a place there, but they would go to church or theater together, and they were much addicted to luncheons. She would come down town at noon to meet him, and then— what banquets! Sometimes they would visit the restaurants where there were fine things, and he would seek to make of her a gourmet. He taught her the beauties of the bobolink in his later attractive form, the form he assumes when, after having been transformed into a reed bird, he comes back on ice to the region where, in the midsummer, he disported himself, and stirs the heart of the good liver, as in June he did the heart of the poet. He taught her the difference between Roquefort cheese, that green garden of toothsome fungi, that crumbly, piquant apotheosis of the best that comes from curd, and all other cheeses, and taught, too, the virtues of each in its own way. She learned the adjuncts of black coffee and hard crackers. She even learned to criticise a claret, and once, with Harlson, she tested a *pousse cafe*, but only once. He didn't approve of it, he said, for ladies. And, besides, a *pousse cafe* was not of merit in itself. It was but a thing spectacular.

And in the matter of made dishes from the man about town she acquired much wisdom.

The man in his great happiness was buoyant and fantastic, and well it was that the woman, too, possessed the sense of humor which makes the world worth occupancy, and that the two could understand together. He was but a foolish boy in this, his delicious period of probation.

And she was but a loving woman who had given her heart to him, who understood him, and who, in a woman's way, was of his mood. It was an idyl of the clever.

At the more modest restaurants were the lunches of these two the most delightful. He would, somehow, find queer little places where all was clean and the cooking good, but far away from the haunts of men, that is, far away from the haunts of the men and women they knew, and there the two would have great feasts. At one unpretending place he had one day found pork and beans,—not the molasses-colored abomination ordinarily sold in town, but the white beans, baked in a deep pan, with the slashed piece of pork browned in the middle of the dish,—and this place became a great resort for them. They would sit at a small table, and have the beans brought on, and mustard of the sharpest and shrewdest, and dishes such as formed a halo about the beans, which were the central figure, and then would they eat, being healthy, and look into each other's face, and riot in present happiness, having certain brains and being in love. The very rudeness of it pleased him mightily.

One evening they had dined together. She had been shopping or doing what it is that women do down town of afternoons, and he had met her at the close of business, and they had eaten together as usual, and when they emerged into the open air it was but to learn that the mercury had dropped some few degrees, and that the jacket she wore was light for the occasion. She became cold before her home was reached, and he was troubled.

"I wish it were months later," he said.

"Why?"

"Because then I could care for you, and see to it that you did not suffer from the chill. I don't know though, even with the admirable supervision I'd have over you then, whether you would take proper care of yourself, my Brownie. What would you do?"

"I don't know quite," she answered. "I think I should want to get pretty near the grate. I'd pull one of the tiger-skins or bear-skins on the rug, very close to the fire, and I'd curl down on the fur and turn about a little, and get very warm."

He assumed a lofty air, and announced that he was under the impression that, when chilled, she would do nothing of the sort! He had his own ideas regarding the treatment of chills of small, brown women. What would really occur, what the solid, tangible fact of the occasion would be, required no effort to describe. He should merely draw a great easy-chair before the grate. Then some one would be picked up and turned about before the fire until thoroughly warmed and with full circulation of the blood again. She should be simply, but scientifically, toasted: "I'd hold you thus before the brand, To catch caloric blisses, And you should be my muffin and I'd butter you with kisses."

She responded that the gift of doggerel was not one to be desired, and, furthermore, that she was not a muffin, nor anything in the culinary way.

All of which, of course, served but as provocation to further flippancy, and, for days later, the lady was referred to as his own sweetest soda biscuit, his bun, his precious fruit-cake, and so on, until a bakery's terms were so exhausted. All this was, no doubt, silliness.

The woman, in her way, was not less inexcusable than the man. She was as much in love as he, and the strictly personal equation was as strong within her. She would watch him when they were at lunch together, and if her gaze was not so bold and feeding as was his, it was at heart as earnest.

She wanted to do something, because of the passionately loving mood within her. She wanted to "hurt" him just a little, and one day occurred an odd thing.

They were chatting across a little table in a restaurant almost vacant save for them, and he had made some grotesque sweetheart comment which had pleased her fancy, lovingly alert, and she suddenly straightened in her seat and looked at him with eyes which were becoming dewy, but said never a word.

She looked all about the room in one swift, comprehensive glance, and then, leaning over, with her small right hand she smote him hardly upon the cheek. There was no occasion for such demonstration. It was but the outpouring, the sweet, barbaric fancy of the woman, in line with the man's grotesquerie, and not one whit less affectionate. And he, thus smitten, made no remonstrance nor defense, further than to refer incidentally to his slender sweet assailant as "a burly ruffian."

That evening, at her home, he suddenly, just before leaving, picked up the woman, as if she were a baby, and threatened to carry her away with him. She did not appear alarmed, at least to the extent of hysteria, though she struggled feebly, and said that somebody was a big, brutal gorilla, and that she did not propose to be snatched from the bosom of her tribe to be conveyed to some tree-top refuge, and there become a monster's bride.

He would assert at times, and the idea was one he clung to with great persistency, that the person with him was not even of the race, but had been substituted in the cradle for a white child stolen by an Indian woman with some great wrong to avenge. He would call her his Chippewa Changeling, and at lunch would be most solicitous as to whether or not the Wild Rose would have a little more of the chicken salad. Would the Flying Pawn try the celery? Some of the jelly, he felt confident, would please the palate of the Brown Dove. Might the white hunter help her to a little more of this or that? Only once she rebelled. She was laughing at something he had said, and he referred to her benignantly as his Minnegiggle, which was, admittedly, an outrage.

A great fancy of these two it was to imagine themselves a couple apart from the crowd, and unversed in city ways, and just from the country. Not from the farm would they come, but from some town of moderate size, for they prided themselves on not being altogether ignorant. Far from it. Was there not a city hall in Blossomville, and a high-school, and were there not social functions there? But, of course, it was a little different in a great city, and it would be well not to mingle too recklessly with the multitude.

They would even visit the circus when one of those "aggregations" made the summer hideous, and he would buy her peanuts and observe all the conventional rules laid down for rural deportment on such occasions. The whimsicality, the childishness of it all, gave it a charm. They appreciated anything together. Harlson said, one day:

"I believe that an old proverb should be changed. 'He laughs best who laughs last,' is incorrect. It should be: 'He laughs best who laughs with some one else.' And that is what will make us strong in life, my love. Some trying times may come, but we shall be brave. We'll just look at each other, and laugh, because we shall understand. We know. We, somehow, comprehend together. Don't you see? Of course you do, because, if you didn't understand, what I am saying would be nonsense."

She understood well enough. She understood his very heartbeats. It had grown that way.

"I am getting very much like you, I think," she said, "and I want you to understand, sir, that I do not regret it. I'm afraid I'm lost totally. I'm not alarmed that it is as if your blood were in my veins. What can a poor girl do?"

"You might as well abandon yourself," he answered. "What is it they do in a part of Africa, when something to last forever is intended? I think they drink a little of another's blood. Could you do that?"

She laughed. "I could drink yours."

He bared his arm in an instant, and sank the point of a penknife into a small vein. The red current came out upon the smooth skin prettily. She looked at Harlson's act in astonishment, and turned a little pale; then, all at once, with a great resolve in her eyes, she bent swiftly forward and applied the red of her lips to that upon the arm. She raised her head proudly, and he looked at her delightedly.

"How did it taste?"

"Salty"—with a pucker of her lips and a desperate effort to keep from fainting.

"Yes, there is much saline matter in blood. Even such admirable blood as that you have just tasted is, no doubt, a little salty. Are you sorry you did it?"

"No," she said, bravely, but she was pallid still.

"Allow me to remind you that science has learned many things, and that you will have, literally, some of my blood in your veins. Not much, it is true, but there will be a little."

She replied that she was glad of it.

And henceforth, when her moods most pleased his lordship, he would comment on the good effect of the experiment, and when they differed he would regret that she had not taken more of him.

They were two fools.

CHAPTER XXI

"MY LITTLE RHINOCEROS-BIRD"

It was not all sweet nonsense, though, with this man and woman. Some practical things of life became theirs soon, because of the love which was theirs.

A curious thing, and to me a pleasant thing, occurred one night. I was with Grant Harlson in his room, and he was lying on a sofa smoking, while I lounged in an easy-chair. Harlson was pretty well fagged out, for it was the end of a hard day for him, as, for that matter, it had been for me. There was a ward to be carried against a ring, and Harlson was in the midst of the fray for half a hundred reasons, and I was aiding him. He headed the more reputable faction, but in the opposition were many shrewd men and men of standing.

It was no simple task we had before us, and we had been working hard, and we were not quite satisfied with the condition of things. The relations of two men of prominence we wanted to know particularly. Had there, or had there not, been a coalition between them? If there had, it would change Harlson's policy, naturally, but work so . far had been conducted on the supposition that an ancient political feud between the two was not yet ended, and that upon the support of one against the other he could count with reasonable certainty. We were discussing this very matter when there came a ring at the door, and a cab-driver entered.

"There is a lady in my cab," said he, "who wants to see Mr. Harlson."

Harlson was puzzled.

"I don't know what it means," he said. "Come down with me and we'll solve the mystery," and we went to where the cab was drawn close to the sidewalk.

The door was opened with some energy, and a woman's head appeared—a head with brown hair.

"Grant!"

"Jean! What is the matter? What brings you here at such a time? My poor child."

She laughed. "There is nothing the matter, you big baby. Only I heard something I thought you would care to know, and which I thought you should know at once, so I came to tell you."

"Yes, tell me."

"It was this way, you see." All this impetuously. "I was at Mrs. Carlson's party, and among the guests were Mr. Gordon and Mr. Mason, with their wives. I didn't listen intentionally, of course, but Mr. Mason and Mr. Gordon came close to where I was sitting and I heard your name mentioned, and I suppose that made my hearing suddenly acute, and I heard in two sentences enough to know that those two gentlemen are working together against you in something political. So, sir, knowing your foolish interest in such things, and actuated by my foolish interest in you, I told aunt I'd like to go home early, and a cab was called and I was put into it, and I told the driver to come here, and—you know the rest, you staring personage."

Women can read men's faces, and Jean Cornish must have

been repaid for what she had done by the mere look of the man before her. He said nothing for a moment, and then uttered only these words softly:

"My little rhinoceros-bird."

"Will you kindly explain the meaning of that extraordinary phrase?"

He did not answer just then, but got into the cab with her and directed the driver to her home.

She had removed her wraps in the drawing-room when she turned to him and demanded further information as to the term applied to her. He made comment on some people's general ignorance of natural history, took a big arm-chair, placed the young lady in a low seat close beside him, and, assuming a ponderous, pedagogical air, began:

"The rhinoceros, my child, as you may possibly be aware, is a huge beast of uncouth appearance, with a horn on its nose, and inhabiting the wild regions of certain wild countries, notably Africa. It is a dangerous animal, and has enemies galore and friends but few. The hunter counts it a noble prize, and steals upon it in its fastnesses, and even a rhinoceros may not withstand the explosive bullet of modern science. Somewhat sluggish and dull, at times, is the rhinoceros, and it is in his careless, listless moods that he is liable to fall a victim. Well for him is it on such occasions that he has a friend, a guardian, a tiny lover. Well for him that the rhinoceros-bird exists! The rhinoceros-bird is a little thing which never deserts the mighty beast. It perches upon his head or back, and flutters about him, and makes of him its world. To the rhinoceros-bird the rhinoceros is all there is of earth. And well is the brute repaid for liking the bird about him. Though the monster may have stupid periods, the bird has none, and, hovering about bushes, fluttering over openings, ever alert, watchful and solicitous, naught may escape its eye, and, danger once discovered, swift is the warning to the slumbering giant, and then woe to the intruder on his domain! And such, dear pupil, is the rhinoceros-bird. And you are my rhinoceros-bird."

She understood, of course. The look in her eyes told that, but her words belied her.

She said that, in a general way, the simile had application, the rhinoceros being a huge beast of uncouth appearance.

And, so far as this conversation was concerned, he perished miserably.

But that was only the beginning of a practical exhibition of the woman's earnestness and acuteness, and her great love. It was but evidence that she was to be, what she became in time, his rhinoceros-bird in all things, his right hand, prompter in such relations as a woman's wit and woman's way best serve. She was of him. But with two who blended, so there must be many added intervals of delicious nonsense before the reality of marriage came.

They made odd names for things. They ate lobster together one day, and he, in some mood, kept misquoting and distorting passages from the Persian poet, and thenceforth broiled lobster was known to the two as "a Rubaiyat." And there were a score or two of other bizarre titles they had made for things or for localities, with the instinct of so embalming a perfect recollection. And each had certain tricks of speech, of course, as have all human beings, and these two, so living in each other, caught all these, and mocked and gibed and imitated, until there was little difference in their pronunciations. To some one overhearing them they might have been deemed as of unsound mind, though they were only talking in love's volapuk.

They resembled each other, these two beings, as nearly in bodily fancies as in other ways. Each, for instance, was a great water lover, each addicted to the bath and perfumes, he perhaps because of his long gymnasium training, and she from the instinct of all purity which appertains to all women worth the owning.

One afternoon they had fled from the city and were walking on the beach, beside the lake, with no one near them. For a mile in either direction, they could look up and down and see that no intruder was in sight. He sent flat stones skipping and galloping over the waves with some whirling trick of underthrow, and tried to teach her the device of it, and they sat upon the sand and ate the luncheon he had secured preparatory to this great excursion, a luncheon devised with great skill by a great caterer, and packed in a paper box which would go in a coat-pocket, and they talked of many things and delighted in being together, and alone. And he, floundering in the sand, must needs get much of it inside his shoe. And then this reckless person, having removed the shoe to rid himself of the sand, must needs step in a treacherous spot and wet his stocking dismally. And the sensible thing to do was to remove the stocking and dry it in the sun.

There should be, so far as its relation to society is concerned, no difference between the human hand and the human foot, but, somehow, the average man is not, as a rule, ready to exhibit his bare feet carelessly to the one woman, and to the average woman a similar revelation would seem a thing indelicate; but these two were not of the common sort. Harlson pulled off his stocking as carefully as he would have done a glove, and spread it on the sand where it might dry, and, laughing at his disaster, he dabbled with his foot in the sand.

She looked at him curiously. She looked at the foot, too, being a woman, and this being the man above all others to her, and then she laughed out joyously and frankly.

"I don't believe any one but you would have done that, Grant. And what a foot you have!"

He replied, with much pomposity, that it was the far-famed

Arabian foot, the instep of which arched so beautifully that water could flow beneath it without wetting the skin. Just at present, though, he thought a little water might run over it to advantage, instead of under, the sand being a trifle mucky. And why would no one else have done such a thing? And he was glad she liked his foot; in fact, he was glad she liked anything about him, and rather wondered that she did, and the world had become to him a good place to live in.

All of which was but the sentimentalism which appertains to a man and a woman in love with each other, but the drift of thought continued in the direction suggested by his action and her comment. They looked at the lake, with its shifting coloring of green and blue and purple, and he told her how, some day, he would teach her to swim like a Sandwich Island beauty, and she said she would like to learn. She liked the water.

"I'm very glad of that," he commented; "I like it myself. I am a great bather. I admire the English for the 'tubbing' which is made such a subject of jest against them by other people. There must be water into which I may tumble when I rise in the morning, or water in abundance in some way, else I should be a trifle uncomfortable all day long. I don't mean just a mild lavatory business, you know, but a plunge or a cataract, or something of that sort. It is barely possible, my dear, that you are going to marry a man whose remote ancestors were the product of evolution from otters, instead of monkeys. Think of that!"

And she confessed, half-blushingly, her own regard for water, and that she had been laughed at by other women for what they deemed a fancy carried to an extreme. And she said she was very glad that a great big Somebody was dainty in his ways. While in many respects she could not approve of him, it was a comfort, at least, to be enabled to think of him as ever clean and wholesome, and as having one weakness of which she could condone.

He looked at her majesty, as she sat enthroned upon a little mound, but to her small oration made no reply. He was worshiping her bodily. And from this conversation came a sequel, a day or two later, which was but the worshiping put into things material. Of his love and the bath he would have fancies, and he wanted what touched her to be from him. She was surprised by a cumbrous package which, opened, revealed great things for a woman's dalliance with water—the soft Turkish towel, vast enough to envelop her, the perfumed soaps, and even the bath-mittens. And she was a little frightened, maybe, at the personality of it all, but she recognized the nature of his fancy, and but loved him the more because he had it. It was an odd gift, it is true, but they were odd people. They were very close together.

An eventful day in other respects, that is, from a lover's point of view, was this one of the outing by the lake. The stocking dried, and in its proper place upon the foot, and inside the shoe again, and the lunch dispatched, there was more idle rambling by the lakeside, and, of course, more lovers' talk. At one place there was a little wood which extended to the water's edge, and there she perched herself in a seat formed by the bent limb of an upturned tree, and he produced from his coat-pocket a paper of macaroons for her dessert, and she sat there munching them like a monkey, while he sprawled, again upon the sand. She made a pretty picture, this small, brown woman, thus exalted; to him a wonderful one. Suddenly she ceased her munching and spoke to him imperiously:

"Come here, sir."

He rose and went to her, standing before her, obedient and waiting. She reached up and took his face between her hands, and pulled his face gently downward until the faces of the two were close together. She looked into his eyes.

"I merely called you up, sir," she said, "to impart a certain piece of information. I am in love with you."

CHAPTER XXII

TWO FOOLS STILL

When a woman, who is all there is in the world to a man, falls into the deliciously generous mood of abandonment, and is revealing what is in her heart, the man, I understand from various excellent authorities, gets about as near heaven as he may ever do in the flesh. And Harlson formed no exception to the rule. The small personage on the limb of the fallen tree owned him as absolutely and completely as ever Cleopatra owned a slave, or Elizabeth a servitor.

"I don't know what to say," he murmured. "There aren't any words—but—you understand."

She pulled his face still closer and kissed him on the lips, though blushing as she did so, for this young woman had fancies regarding lips and regarding kisses which should be entertained by a greater number of the women of the land. Then she told him to lie upon the sand again; that she wanted to look at him. And he obeyed, machine-like.

She was in a fantastic mood assuredly. She watched him, her cheek resting upon one little hand for a long time, a thoughtful look upon her face. Then she broke out impetuously:

"How smooth and clean your face is! Do you—do you go to—you know what I mean. Do you go to a barber every day?"

He answered that he shaved himself.

"Is it very hard?" she asked.

"Well, that depends."

She studied once more for a long time, then spoke again, on this occasion blushing furiously:

"Grant, dear, I want to *do* things for you always. I want to take care of you. It seems to me that, some time, I might learn, you know. It seems to me that some time I might almost"—with a little gasp—"shave you."

He wanted to gather her up in his arms and smother and caress her, after that climax of tender admission, but she waved her hand as she saw him rising. He fell back then upon his ignoble habit of talking vast science to her.

"My dear, that dream may, I hope, be realized. I'd rather have my face slashed by you than be shaved by the most careful, conscientious and silent barber in all Christendom, but shaving is a matter of much gravity. It is not the removal of the beard which tests the intellect; it is the sharpening of the razors."

"How is that, sir?"

"All razors are feminine, and things of moods. The razor you sharpen to-day may not be sharp, though manipulated upon hone or strap with all persistence and all skill. The razor you sharpen to-morrow may be far more tractable. Furthermore, the razor which is comparatively dull to-day may be sharp to-morrow, without further treatment."

She said that, in her opinion, that was nonsense, and that he was trying to impose upon a friendless girl, because the topic was one of which men would, ordinarily, have a monopoly, and regarding which they would assume all wisdom, and, perhaps, make jests.

"I am in earnest," he said. "Razors have moods, and are known to sulk. But science has solved the conundrum of their antics. It has been discovered that whetting changes the location of the molecules of metal, that there is frequently left what is not a perfect edge after the supposed sharpening, but that, given time, the molecules will readjust themselves, and the edge return. My dear, you are now, or at least should be, a woman rarely learned in one great mystery. Is there no reward for merit?"

She scorned reply to such a screed, but slid down from her perch with the remark that she had "et hearty." A man who had eaten near them in a restaurant had used the expression, and they had both promptly adopted it.

He rose, went to her side, and leaned over, and inhaled the perfume of her hair.

She looked up mischievously. "You are a big black animal!"

As already remarked, these two were very foolish.

That same evening, when Grant Harlson reached his office, he found a note awaiting him. It was a pretty, perfumed thing, and he knew the handwriting upon it well. He had not seen the writer for three months. He had almost forgotten her existence, yet she had been one with whom his life had been, upon a time, closely associated. He opened the envelope and read the note:

MY DEAR GRANT: Yon know I am philosophical—for a woman—and that I have never been exacting. I have formed habits, though, and have certain foolish ways. One of these ways was to be much with Grant Harlson, not very long ago. I lost him, somehow, but still have a curiosity to see his face again, to note if it has changed. I have something to say to him, too. Please call upon me to-night. ADA.

The effect of the note upon the man was not altogether pleasant. He felt a certain guiltiness at his own indifference. This clever woman of the social world he knew was not to be trifled with by one unarmored or irresolute. He had hoped she would forget him, that his own indifference would breed the same feeling upon her part, and now he knew he was mistaken, as men have been mistaken before. There was an interview to be faced, and one promising interesting features. He started on the mission with a grimace.

CHAPTER XXIII

JUST A PANG

Mrs. Gorse was at home, the servant said, and Harlson found her awaiting him in a room which was worth a visit, so luxurious were its appointments and so delicate its colorings and its perfumes. A woman of admirable taste was Mrs. Gorse, and one who knew how to produce dramatic effect. But dramatic effects as between her and Grant Harlson were things of the past. People sometimes know each other so well that the introduction of anything but reality is absurd. Mrs. Gorse attempted nothing as Harlson entered. She was not posed. She was standing, and met him at the door smilingly.

"How do you do, Grant?"

"I'm well," he said, "and how are you? Certainly you are looking well."

"I am not ill. I think I am not plumper nor more thin than usual. I imagine my weight is normal."

He laughed.

"And how much is that?"

The woman flushed a little.

"It is hardly worth the telling, since you do not remember.

There was a time, you know, when you had some whim about it, and when I had to report to you. You professed to be solicitous about my health or personal appearance, or whatever it was that led you to the demand. And you have forgotten."

He was uneasy. "That is true, Ada. I did have that fad, didn't I? Well, I forget the figures, but I see that you are still yourself, and as you should be."

She shrugged her shoulders. "Take the big chair. It's the one you like best. You see I don't forget certain trifles" (this with a slight trembling inflection). "And tell me about yourself. I haven't seen you for three months and over. Haven't you been out of town. Couldn't you have written me a note."

"I've not been out of town. I might have written you a note, but I didn't suppose it mattered."

"Yet there is a legend to the effect that men and women sometimes get to be such friends, and have such relations, that a sudden unexplained absence of three months matters a great deal."

"That is so. But—what is the use, Ada? It doesn't matter with us, does it? Are we not each capable of taking care of ourselves? Were we ever of the conventionally sentimental?"

She sighed. "I suppose not. But it grew that way a little, didn't it, Grant? Has it all been nothing to you?"

"I won't say that," he answered. "It has been a great deal to me, but isn't it wiser to make all in the past tense now? What have we to gain?"

She tried to smile. "Nothing, I suppose." Then breaking out fiercely: "You are a strange man! You are like the creature Margrave, in Bulwer's hard 'Strange Story,' with mind and body, but with no soul nor sympathy."

The man in his turn became almost angry. He spoke more grimly:

"You are not just! Have I broken any pledge or violated any promise, even an implied one? Have we not known each other on even terms? It was but a pact for mutual enjoyment until either should be weary. We have no illusions. You a Lilith of the red earth, not of Adam; you a woman sweet and passionate and kind, but soulless, too, and fickle; and I a trained man, made as soulless by experience, we met and agreed, without words, to break a lance in a flirtation. And that both lances were splintered doesn't matter now. We had joy in the encounter, didn't we, and more after each surrendered captive? But it has been only mimic warfare. It has not been the real thing."

"Evidently not—to you! Unfortunately one forgets sometimes, and then one is endangered."

He was troubled. He rose and came to her side, and put his hand upon her head, the usually proudly carried head of a handsome woman, now bowed in the effort to hide a face which told too much. "It is all unfortunate. It is unfortunate that we met, if you care as you profess. I had counted us as equal; that you were, with me, caring for the day and never for the morrow, so far as we two were concerned."

She raised her face. "Do you love me?" she said.

He hesitated. "I am fond of you."

"Do you love me?"

"In the sense that I suppose you mean, no."

She did not look at him for a moment; then she rose swiftly to her feet and looked squarely in his face.

"Is there some one else?"

He did not answer.

"Is there some one else?"

"Yes."

"Then it *is* unfortunate, as you say—and for her."

"What do you mean?"

"I mean that I will not endure to be dropped by you as a child drops a toy of which it is weary. I mean that I will not surrender you to some new creature who has intervened! What does it matter that there has been no pledge between us? You have made me love you! You know it! The very being to each other what you and I have been is a pledge for the future. Oh, Grant!"

The woman's eyes were full of tears, and her voice was a moan. The man was suffering both shame and agony. He knew that, careless as he had been, the relations had grown to imply a permanency. The woman was at least justified in her claims that words are not always necessary to a contract. What could he do? Then came the thought of Jean. One hair of her brown head was more to him than this woman, or any other woman he had ever known. He was decided.

"I am a brute, Ada," he said, "or, at least, I have to be brutal. We do care for each other in a certain way, and we have found together many of the good things in living, but we are not lovers in the greater sense. We never could be. It means much. means a knitting together of lives, a oneness, a confluence of soul and heart and passions, and a disposition to sacrifice, if need be. We have not been that way, and are not. We have been more like two chess-players. We have had a mutual pleasure in the game, but we have been none the less antagonists. The playing is over, that is all. It doesn't matter who has won the game. We will call it drawn, or you may have it. But it is ended!"

She stood with one hand upon her breast. There came a shadow of pain to her face, and a hard look followed.

"It is nonsense talking about the game. The playing ended a year ago, and you were the winner. Now you are careless about the prize! Well" (bitterly), "it may not be worth much—to you."

"It is worth a great deal. It has been worth a great deal to me. But I must relinquish it."

"Why did you make me care for you?" she demanded, fiercely, again.

"I did not do more than you did. As I said before, we played the game together. It is but the usual way of a flirting man and woman. We should have each been more on guard."

The woman was silent for a little time, and it was evident that she was making an effort at self-control. She succeeded. She had half-turned her back to Harlson, and when she again faced him, she had assumed her dignity.

"You are right, after all," she said. "I did not consider your own character well enough. You tire of things. You will tire of the woman you love now. And you will come back to me, just because I have been less sentimental, and, so, less monotonous than some others. Whether or not I shall receive you time will determine. Is that the way you want me to look at it?"

He bowed. "That is perhaps as good a way as any. It doesn't matter. Will you shake hands, Ada?"

She reached out her hand listlessly, and he took it. A minute later nd he was on the street. And so the last link of one sort with the past was broken. It was long—though he had no concealments from her—before he told Jean of this interview. And then he did not tell the woman's name, nor did she care to know.

CHAPTER XXIV

AS TO THOSE OTHERS

Time passes, even with an impatient lover, and so there came an end at last to Grant Harlson's season of probation. There was nothing dramatic about the wedding.

To him the ceremony was merely the gaining of the human title-deed to the fortune which was his on earth, and to Jean Cornish it was but the giving of herself fully to the man—that which she wished to do with herself. There were few of us present, but we were the two's closest friends. They were a striking pair as they stood together and plighted their faith calmly: he big and strong, almost to the point of burliness, and she slight, sweet and lissom. There was no nervousness apparent in either, perhaps because there was such earnestness. And then he carried her away from us.

They had not been long away, this newly wedded couple, when they returned to the home he had prepared. As he remarked half grimly to me, in comment on lost years, they had met so late in the nesting season that time should not be wasted. Of that home more will be told in other pages, but it is only of the two people I am talking now.

I noted a difference in their way when I first dined with them, which I did, of course, as soon as they had returned. I had thought them very close together before in thought and being, but I saw that there was more. The sweet, sacred intimacy which marriage afforded had given the greater fullness to what had seemed to me already perfect. But I was one with much to learn of many things. And yet these two were to come closer still—closer through a better mutual understanding and new mutual hopes. It was long afterward when I understood.

It was after dinner one day, and in the sitting-room, which was a library as well. They were going out that evening, but it was early still, and he was leaning back in a big chair smoking the post-prandial cigar, and she coiled upon a lower seat very near him, so near that he could put his hand upon her head, and they were talking lightly of many things. She looked up more earnestly at last.

"Will you ever tire of it, Grant?"

He laughed happily.

"Tire of what, Brownie?"

"Of this, of me, and of it all; will you never weary of the quietness of it and want some change? You must care very much, indeed, if you will not."

He spoke slowly.

"It seems to me that though we were to live each a thousand years, I would never tire of this as it is. But, of course, it will not be just this way. We could not keep it so if we would, and would not if we could."

"Why should it change?"

He drew her close to him and placed his hand upon her face and kissed her on the forehead.

"I shall be more in the fray again. I must be. You would not have your husband a sluggard among men, and that will sometimes take me from you, though never for long, because

I'm afraid I shall be selfish and have you with me when there are long journeys. And it will change, too, you know—because you see, dear, there may be the—the others. You hope so, with me, do you not?"

Her face remained hidden for a little time. When she raised it, there was a blush upon her cheeks, but her eyes had not the glance he had anticipated.

"No!" she said.

He did not reply, because he could not comprehend. He looked at her, astonished, and she broke forth recklessly:

"I love you so, Grant! I love you so! I want you, just you, and no one else. Are we not happy as we are? Are you not satisfied with me, just me? You are like all men! You are selfish! You— oh, love! You love me so—I know that—but you think of me—it seems so, anyhow—as but part of a scheme of life, of the life which will make you happy. My love, my husband! why need it be that way? Why am I not enough? Why may we not be one, just one, and be that way? I want nothing more. Why should you? Are we not all our own world? I will be everything to you. Oh, Grant!" And she ceased, sobbingly.

The man said nothing. He could not understand at first; then came upon him, gradually, a comprehension of how different had been their dreams in some ways. It was inexplicable. He thought of the mother instinct which gives even to the little girl a doll. He had supposed that his own fancies were but weak reflections of what was in the innermost heart of the woman he loved so. He blurted out, almost roughly:

"'Portia is Brutus' harlot, not his wife." Then added, bitterly, "It is the man who is saying it this time, you see."

A second later, shame-faced and repentant, he had caught the slender figure in his arms and was holding it close to him.

"I'm a brute, dear," he said, "and there is no excuse for me. I understand, I think. We dreamed differently. That was all. Had you loved me less, dear heart, you would have been more like other women. But it doesn't matter. It shall be as you say, as you may wish or fancy. We thought unlike, yet you were as much the pivot of my thought as I of yours. It was of you, for you, and because of you, I had my visions. That is all. And we will not talk more of it."

She nestled closer to him, and he stroked the brown mass of her hair and remained silent. Some moments passed that way. Then she roused herself and sat up squarely, and looked him bravely in the face.

"I have been thinking," she said, "and I can think very well when I am so close to you, with my head where it is now. I have been thinking, and it has occurred to me that I was not a wise, good woman, and I want you to forgive me."

His answer involved no words at all, but it was meet for every purpose. She pushed him away from her, and spoke gravely:

"Will you do something for me, Grant?"

"Yes."

"Will you do it now?"

"Yes—if it be good for you."

"I want you to do this. I want you to imagine me some one else, some one you regard, but for whom you do not care particularly. And then I want you to tell me what you think, what you would think best about the—'the others'"—blushing more fairly than any rose that ever grew on stem. "Will you do that?"

His face was very earnest. "I will try," he said, "but it will be difficult to imagine you someone else. How can I do that when

I can look into your eyes, my little wife? I'll try, though."

"Then talk to me, now."

He was troubled. He did not know how to express himself in the spirit asked of him, and he did not look at her in the beginning.

"Sweetheart, you are a part of me, and you are the greatest of what there is of my life. It is about you that all my thoughts converge. I do not suppose there will be any happier, any dearer time ever than this we are passing together, with none to molest us, or divert us from each other. You know me well now. I am what I am, and never was a man of stronger personal moods or one who so hungered for the one woman. And you are the one woman, the one physical object in the world, I worship. There is no need that I tell you anything. And you have learned, too, how I care for you in all greater, and, it may be, purer ways. We are happy together. But, love of me, we are a man and wife, an American man and wife, of the social grade—for there are social grades, despite all our democracy—where, it seems to me, a family has come to be esteemed almost a disgrace, as something vulgar and annoying. And it seems to me this is something unnatural, and all wrong. Whatever nature indicates is best. To do what nature indicates is to secure the greatest happiness. Trials may come, new sorrows and incumbrances be risked, but nature brings her recompense. I want you the mother of our child, of our children, as it may be. I know what your thought has been, I understand it now, but how can children separate us? When a man and woman look together upon a child, another human being, a part of each of them, a being who would never have existed had they not found each other, a being with the traits of each combined, it seems to me as if their souls should blend somehow as never before. They are one then, to a certainty. They have become a unit in the great scheme of existence. And so, darling, I have thought and thought much. I have dreamed of you as the little mother, the one who would not be of the silly modern type, the one who, with me, would not be ashamed any more than were our sturdy ancestors of a sturdy family, should we be blessed so. The one who would be glad with me in the womanhood and manhood of it. And, as I said, it could never part us. It would but make me more totally your own, more watchful, if that were possible, more tender, if that could be, more worshipful of you in the greater life of us two together, us two more completely. And that is all. It shall be as you say, and I will not complain, for I know your impulse in what you said and all its lovingness."

She had listened to each word intently, and her face had flushed and paled alternately. When he had done she snuggled more closely to him, and still said nothing. When she did speak, this is what she said, and she said it earnestly:

"I was wrong, my husband; I was a selfish, infatuated woman, who loved with one foolish idea which marred its fullness. You have taught me something, dear. You could not give me the thought I had again, even were you to try yourself, for I see it now. And—"

She put her arms about his neck and buried her fair face upon the pillow which afforded her such convenient shelter. As for the man, there was something like a lump in his throat, but he spoke with an effort at playfulness, though his voice wavered a little:

"It is right, my love. And we will visit this nature of ours together. It is the season now, and next week we go camping. I want to show old friends of mine, the spirits of the forest, how fair a wife I've won."

And, a few days later, there was a pretty little scene down town. "Sportsmen's Goods," the sign above the doorway said, and in the windows were numerous wooden ducks and dainty rods of split bamboo, and glittering German silver reels and gaudy flies, and a thousand things to delight the heart of a fisherman or hunter. Enter, a broad-shouldered gentleman and a haughty wisp of a woman, the latter a trifle embarrassed, despite her stateliness.

"How are you, Jack?"

This to the proprietor of the place, as he comes forward.

"How are you, Harlson?"

"This is Mrs. Harlson." The ceremony takes place. "Now, Jack, here's a grave matter of business. Have you a private room? And I want you to send in a lot of light wading-boots— the smallest sizes. And I want some other things." And the list is given.

And the lady and gentleman disappear into a small room assigned them, and a lot of wading-boots are taken in, and time elapses. And, eventually, lady and gentleman emerge again, the man's eyes full of laughter, and the woman's eyes full of laughter and confusion, and a package is made up.

"Send it to my house, Jack," says the man, and the couple leave the place.

CHAPTER XXV

MATURE AGAIN

Michigan is divided into two peninsulas, the apexes of which meet.

The State is shaped like an hour-glass, with the upper portion twisted to the left. About all the two peninsulas lie blue waters, the inland seas, lakes Michigan, Superior and Huron. Upon the upper peninsula are great mineral ranges, copper and iron, a stunted but sturdy forest growth, and hundreds of little lakelets. The lower peninsula, at its apex, is yet largely unclaimed from nature, but, toward the south, broadens out into the great area of grain and apple blossoms, and big, natty towns, once the country of oak openings, the haunt of Pontiac and of Tecumseh, braided and crossed by one of Cooper's romances.

It is with the crest of the lower peninsula that this description deals. There exist not the rigors of the northern peninsula; there the timber has not tempted woodland plunderers, nor have dried brook-beds followed shorn forests, nor the farmer invaded the region of light soil. There is the dense but stunted growth of the hard maple and pine and beech and fir, and there are windfalls and slashes which sometimes bridge the creeks. There are still black ash swales and dry beech ridges, but they are not as massive as further south. There are still the haunting deer and the black bear and the ruffed grouse, the "partridge" in the idiom of the country, the "pheasant" of the

South and Southwest. There are scores of tiny lakes, deep and pure and tenanted, and babbling streams, and there are the knighted speckled trout, the viking black bass and that rakish aristocrat, the grayling.

One way to cross from Michigan to Huron is in a canoe, threading one's way from woodland lake to woodland lake, through brush-hidden brooklets, without a portage. In this region the liverwort blooms fragrantly beside the snow-bank in early spring, and here the arbutus exists as in New England. The adder-tongues and violets and anemones are here in rare profusion in their time, and the wandering gray wolf, last of his kind, almost, treads softly over knolls carpeted with wintergreen and decorated with scarlet berries. It is a country of blue water and pure air, of forest depths and long alleys arching above strong streams.

This is the southern peninsula of Michigan in its northern part, and here came, as the first suspicion of a tinge of yellow came to the leaves of certain trees, as the hard maple trees first flashed out in faint red, two people.

There were three of them who came at first, for there was the man with the wagon, engaged in the outlying settlement, who brought them fifteen miles into the depths of the woodland. They came lumbering through an archway over an old trail, the homesteader sitting jauntily, howbeit uncertainly, upon the front seat—for the roadway tilted in spots—and behind him a couple from the town, a man and a woman, the man laughing and supporting his companion as the wagon swayed, and the woman wondering and plucky, and laughing, too, at the oddness of it all. The forest amazed her a little, and awed her a little, but from awe of it soon came, as they plunged along, much friendliness. She was receptive, this game woman, and knew Nature when she met her.

In the rear of the wagon crouched or stood upright, or laid down, as the mood came upon his chestnut-colored grandness, a great Irish setter, loved of the man because of many a day together in stubble or over fallow, loved of the woman because he, the setter, had already learned to love and regard the woman as an arbitrator, as queen of something he knew not what.

And so the wagon rumbled on and pitched and tilted, and finally, in mid-afternoon, reached a place where the road seemed to end. There was a little open glade, but a few yards across, and there was dense forest all around, and, just beyond the glade, the tree-tops seemed to all be lowered, because there was a descent and a lake half a mile long, as clear as crystal and as blue as the sky. A little way beyond the glade could be heard the gurgling and ruffling of a creek, which, through a deep hollow, came athwart the forest and plunged into the lake most willingly. This was the place where these two people, this man and woman, were to end their present journey, for the man had been there before and knew what there to seek and what to find.

And there was a creaky turn of the wagon, a disembarkment, and an unloading of various things. There was all the kit for a hunter of the northern woods, and there were things in addition which indicated that the hunter was not alone this time. There was a tent which had more than ordinarily selected fixtures to it, and there were two real steamer-chairs with backs, and there were four or five of what in the country they call "comforts," or "comforters," great quilts, thickly padded, generally covered with a design in white of stars or flowers on beaming red, and there were rods and guns and numerous utensils for plain cooking.

The wagon with its horses and its driver turned about and tumbled along the roadway on its return, and there were left alone in the forest, miles from civilization, miles from any human being save the driver fast leaving them, the man and woman and the setter dog.

They did not appear depressed or alarmed by the circumstance.

The load from the wagon had been left in a heap. The man pulled from it a camp-chair with a back, and opened it, and set it up on the grass very near the edge of the glade, and announced that the throne was ready for the Empress, not of Great Britain and India, nor of any other part of the earth, but of the World; it was ready, and would she take her seat?

He explained that, as, at present, there were some things she didn't know anything about, she might as well sit in state. So the Empress, who was not very big, sat in state.

The dog had pursued a rabbit, and was making a fool of himself. The man selected from among the baggage left an ax, heavy and keen, and attacked a young spruce tree near. It soon fell with a crash, and the Empress leaped up, but to sit down again and look interestedly at what was going on.

The man, the tree fallen, sheared off its wealth of fragrant tips, and laid the mass of it by the side of the great tree. Then from out the wagon's leavings he dragged a tent, a simple thing, and, setting up two crotched sticks with a cross-pole, soon had it in its place. He carried the mass of spruce-tips by armfuls to the tent and dumped them within it until there was a great heap of soft, perfumed greenness there. Then, over all, he spread a quilt or two, and announced, with much form, to her majesty, that her couch was prepared for her, and that she could sit in the front of the tent if she wished.

And he cut and put in place two more forked stakes, with a cross-bar, and hung a kettle and built a fire beneath, and brought water and got out a frying-pan and bread and prepared for supper. All articles not demanded for immediate use were stowed away just back of the tent. "And," he remarked, "there you are."

The Empress rose from her camp-chair and investigated.

"Are we to sleep in the tent, Grant?"

"Yes."

"What will we do if it rains?"

"Stay in the tent."

"But we'll get wet, won't we?"

"No; we'll be upon the spruce-tops; the water will run under us."

"Aren't there animals in the wood?"

"Yes."

"What will you do if they come about?"

"I think I'll kiss you."

The Empress of the World did not seem to fully enter into the spirit of his carelessness.

She had her imaginings, after all. She knew that she was all right, somehow, yet she did not quite comprehend. But she knew her royalty.

She rose and went to the entrance of the tent, and stepped in daintily, and sat down in another chair which had been placed there for her reception, and then inhaled all the sweetness of the spruce-tips, and pitched herself down upon the quilts, and curled herself up there for a moment or two, and then rose and came out again into the open, where her husband stood watching her.

"Do you like the woods, dear?" he said.

"Don't you see?"

He said nothing, but led her majesty to a seat for a time, while he got ready for the evening meal—of food from the town for his first time—and then, in a courtier's way, of course, suggested, that she aid him.

They cooked and ate the strips of bacon with the soft stale bread he had brought, and drank the tea, and the shadows of the trees lengthened across the glade, and the chestnut-hued setter came back to camp and was gravely reprimanded by his master, and it soon became night, and time passed, and the fire flashed against the greenery strangely, and the man took the woman by the hand and led her to the entrance to the tent, and said:

"We must rise early."

She entered the tent, and not long later he entered, also, or thought to do so. He lifted the flap, which he had let down, and looked inside.

She lay there upon the cushioned spruce-tips, and, as he raised the white curtain, the moonlight streamed in upon her.

She looked up at him, and smiled.

The loving face of her was all he saw—the face of the one woman.

He spoke to her. He tried to tell her what she was to him, and failed. She answered gently and in few words. They understood.

He entered the tent and sat upon the couch beside her as she was lying there, and took her small hand in his, but said no more. From the wood about them—for it was into the night now—came many sounds, known of old, and wonderfully sweet to him, but all new and strange to her.

"Ah-rr-oomp, ah-rr-oomp, ba-rr-oomp," came from the edge of the water the deep cry of the bullfrog; from the further end of the lake came the strange gobble, gurgle and gulp of the shitepoke, the small green heron which is the flitting ghost of shaded creeks and haunting thing of marshy courses everywhere. Night-hawks, far above, cried with a pleasant monotony, then swooped downward with a zip and boom. It was not so late in the season that the call of the whippoorwill might not be heard, and there were odd notes of tree-toads and katydids from the branches. There came suddenly the noise of a squall and scuffle from the marshy edge of the lake, where 'coons were wrangling, and the weird cry of the loon re-echoed up and down. The air was full of the perfumes of the wood. The setter just outside the tent became uneasy, and dashed into a thicket near, and there was a snort and the measured, swift thud of feet flying in the distance. A deer had been attracted by the fire-light. An owl hooted from a dead tree near by. There was the hum of many insects of the night, and the soft sighing of the wind through boughs. It was simply night in the northern woods.

The man rose and went outside, and stood with one hand upon the tent-pole at the front. He seemed to himself to be in a dream. He looked up at the moon and stars, and then at the glittering greenery deepening further out into blackness about him. He looked down toward the grass at his feet, and there appeared near him a flash of gold.

What Harlson saw was but a dandelion. That most home-like and steadfast flower blooms in early springtime and later in the season, with no regard to the chronology of the year. It was one of the vagrant late gladdeners of the earth that his eye chanced to light upon.

It held him, somehow. It was wide open—so wide that there was a white spot in its yellow center—and close above it drooped, a beech-tree's branch, so close that one long green leaf hung just above the petals. And upon this green leaf the dew was gathering.

The man looked at the flower.

"Is all the world golden?" he said to himself. And he straightened and moved and went from the tent to where the open was. He stood in the glade in the moonlight, and wondered at it all.

Here he was—he could not comprehend it—here, all alone, save for her, in the forest, miles away from any other human being! He had wholly loved but two things all his life—her and nature—and the three of them—she, nature and he—were here together! It was wonderful!

And there in that preposterous covering of canvas, half hid in the forest's edge, was Jean Cor—no, Jean Harlson, belonging to him—all his—away from all the world, just part of him, in this solitude!

He wondered why he had deserved it. He wondered how he had won it. He looked up at the pure sky, with the moon defined so clearly, and all the stars, and was grateful, and reached out his hands and asked the Being of it to tell him, if it might be, how to do something as an offset.

The night passed, and the sun rose clearly over the forest. The chestnut setter roused himself from behind the tent, and came in front of it, and barked joyously at a yellow-hammer which had chosen a great basswood tree with deadened spaces for an early morning experiment toward a breakfast.

There issued from the white tent a man, who looked upward toward all the greenness and all the glory, and was glad.

He looked downward at the sward, and there was the little flower. And the dew had run its course, and had gathered in a jewel at the leaf's tip, and there, fallen in the midst of the disk of yellow, was the product from the skies. There, in the flower's heart, was the perfect gem—a diamond in a setting of fine gold!

CHAPTER XXVI

ADVENTURES MANIFOLD

"I've et hearty," said the woman, saucily, as the breakfast, for which the birds furnished the music, was done. And then he initiated her into the brief art of washing tin things in the gravel at the water's edge. Then he informed her that target practice was about to begin, and brought out four guns from their cases.

Two of the pieces were rifles, and of each kind one was a light and dainty piece. He said they would practice with the rifles; that when she became an expert rifle-shot the rest would all be easy, and then upon the boll of a tree at one side of the opening he pinned a red scrap of paper, and shot at it.

With the report half the scrap was torn away, and then he taught her how to hold the piece and how to aim.

She expressed, at last, a desire to shoot, and he gave her the little rifle loaded. She aimed swiftly and desperately, and pressed the trigger, and the echoes had not died away when she let fall the gun upon the grass.

"I'm hurt," she said.

He sprang to her side, pale-faced, as she raised her hand to her shoulder, but he brightened a moment later. He opened the dress at her neck, and turned it down on one side, and there, on the round, white shoulder, was a slight ruddy bruise. He kissed it, and laughed.

"It'll be all right in no time. Now, do as I tell you."

He put a cartridge in the piece again.

"Try it once more," he said; "aim more deliberately and hold the stock of the gun very tightly against your shoulder as you fire."

"But it will hurt me."

"No, it won't. Do as I tell you."

She would have obeyed him had he told her to leap into the lake, and the lake was deep.

She set her lips firmly, held the gun hard against her shoulder, aimed carefully and fired.

The red spot flew from the gray trunk of the oak. She looked up amazed.

"Why, it didn't hurt me a bit!"

"Of course not. There is a law of impact, and you are learning it. The strongest man in the world could not hurt you pushing you against nothing. He could kill you with a blow. With the first shot your gun gave you a blow. In the second it could only push you. Listen to the wisdom of your consort!"

She made a mouth at him, and he told her she'd had her "baptism of fire," and soon they sallied into the forest, hunting.

She was very pretty and piquant in her kilted dress and shooting jacket and high boots. It was a formidable army of two.

There were myriads of bees in the openings, and the fall flowers were yielding up the honey to be stored, in the hearts of great trees, and at noon-time they sat down in one of the openings for luncheon.

He had shot only a couple of ruffed grouse, for it was a ramble rather than a real hunt, this first mid-wood excursion of the pair, and she had shot at various things, a grouse or two and squirrels, and missed with regularity, and was piqued over it, but he had noted her increasing courage and confidence and resolution with each successive shot, and knew that he had with him, for the future, a "little sportsman," as he called her.

They built a fire, just for the fun of it, and a grouse was plucked and broiled with much ado, and never was greater feast. And, the meal over, he produced a cigar and—which was not really good form for the woods—lay on the grass and smoked it, looking at her and talking nonsense.

She sat upon a log and delighted in the fragrance and the light, and the droning sounds and bird-cries, and the new world of it to her. All at once, her gaze became fixed upon some object a little distance away. She reached out her hand to him appealingly.

"What is that?"

He rose and looked where she pointed.

Years of decay had made of the trunk of a fallen tree but a long ridge of crumbling, brown chips, and, upon this ridge, where the sun streamed down hotly, lay something coiled in a black mass, and there was a flat, hideous head resting upon it all with beady eyes which seemed, to leer.

Harlson looked at it carelessly.

"Big one, isn't it?" he said.

"What is it?" she gasped.

"What is it, you small ignoramus! It's a blacksnake and a monster. It is one of the dreads of the small life of the wood, and it was one of the dreads of my youth, and its days are numbered."

He reached for his gun, then checked himself.

"Shoot it."

She picked up the little rifle and raised it to her shoulder, as calmly as any Leather-Stocking in the land.

The report came like a whip-crack, and up from the dead log leaped a great writhing mass, which coiled and twisted and thrashed about, and finally lay still.

Harlson walked up and examined what he called the "remains." Half the serpent's ugly head had been torn away by the bullet.

"It was a great shot! 'And the woman shall bruise the serpent's head!'" he quoted. "Egad, you've done it with a vengeance, my huntress! And you are a markswoman among many, and thy price is above rubies! Hooray!"

She informed him, with much dignity, that she never missed such monsters as were blacksnakes, and that her undoubted skill with the rifle was due to the quality of the tutor she had owned, and, at the same time, would he mind moving to some other place to finish his cigar, for the sight of the dead monster was not a pleasant thing?

And so was accomplished the woman's first feat with the gun; but on that same day, before they had returned to camp, she had slain, at a fair distance, a grouse which, when flushed, had sailed away with lofty contempt for but a score of yards, and, alighting upon a limb close beside the body of a tree, had stood awaiting, jauntily and ignorantly, his doom.

She was a proud woman when the bird came plunging to the ground, and of that particular fowl he remarked, subsequently, when they were eating it, that its flavor was a little superior to anything in the way of game he had ever tasted, and he was more than half in earnest.

And the nights were poems and the days were full of life, and the brown cheeks of the woman became browner still, and she was referred to more frequently than even in the ante-wedded days as merely of the tribe of Chippewas.

In one respect, too, she excelled in deserving that same title, for your Chippewa, of either sex, takes to the water like a duck, as becomes a tribe of the lake regions. He took her to the lake and taught her not to fear it, and they frolicked in its waves together, and she learned to swim as well as he, and to dive as smoothly as a loon or otter, and was a water nymph such as the creatures of the wood had never seen. He was very vain of her art acquired so swiftly, though in conversation he gave vast credit to her teacher. And in the catching of the black bass there came eventually to the nine-ounce split bamboo in her little hands as many trophies as to his heavier lancewood. One day, after she had become at home in the water, and had better luck than he, and was lofty in her demeanor, he upset the boat in deep water, and her majesty was compelled to swim about it with him and assist at one end while he was at the other, in righting it. So mean of spirit was he.

All other things, though, were but the veriest trifle compared with the adventure which came at last. He had made her wise in woodcraft, and she could tell at the lake's margin or along the creek's bed the tracks of the 'coon, like the prints of a baby's foot, the mink's twin pads, or the sharp imprint of the hoofs of the deer. One day another track was noted near the camp, a track resembling that of a small man, shoeless, and Harlson informed her that a bear had been about.

She asked if the black bear of Michigan were dangerous, and he said the black bear of Michigan ate only very bad people, or very small ones.

One afternoon they were some distance from the camp. They had been shooting with fair success, and, returning, had seated themselves in idle mood upon one end of a great fallen trunk, upon which they had just crossed the gully, at the bottom of which a little creek tumbled toward the lake. The gleam of a maple's leaves near by, already turning scarlet, had caught her eye; she had expressed a wish for some of the gaudy beauties, and he had climbed the tree and was plucking the leaves for her, when, suddenly, the woods resounded with the fierce barking of the dog in the direction from which they had just come. He called to her to be ready to shoot, that a deer might have been started, when there was a crashing through the bushes and the quarry burst into sight.

Lumbering into the open, turning only to growl at the dog which was yelping wildly in its rear, but keeping wisely out of its reach, was a black bear. The beast did not see the woman opposite him, but rushed at the log and was half way across it when she screamed. Then it paused. Behind was the dog, before the woman; it advanced slowly, growling.

Harlson, in the tree, saw it all, and, as a fireman drops with a rush down the pole in the engine-house, he came down the maple's boll and bounded toward the log. The bear hesitated.

"Shoot! you little fool, shoot!" shouted the man, as he ran.

Her courage returned in a moment, at least did partial presence of mind. She raised the gun desperately, and the report rang out. The bear clutched wildly at the log, then rolled off, and fell to the rocky bottom, twenty feet below. Harlson seized his own gun and looked down. The beast was motionless, and from a little hole in its head the blood was trickling.

And the woman—well, the woman was sitting on the grass, very pale of face and silent.

The man seized her, and half smothered her with kisses, and shouted aloud to the forest and all its creatures that great was Diana of the Ephesians!

CHAPTER XXVII

THE HOUSE WONDERFUL

And the bear's skin was tanned with the glossy black fur still upon it, the head with the white-fanged jaws still attached and made natural with all the skill of an artist in such things, and it lay, a great, soft, black rug, upon a couch in the House Wonderful, or, at least, the house to which Harlson gave that name. It seemed to him the House Wonderful, indeed.

Therein was held all there was in the world for him, and he was satisfied with it all, and content, save that he felt, at seasons, how little man is worthy of the happiness which may come to him sometimes, even in this world. Yet it was not all poetry in the House Wonderful; there were many practical happenings, and many droll ones.

The House Wonderful, it is needless to say, was in the city. The bear-skin was but one of many such soft trophies of the chase which were spread upon the floors or upon soft lounges and divans. Over this particular skin there was much said, at times, when there were guests.

Jean would explain to some curious person, that she herself had shot the original wearer of the skin, and that her husband was up a tree at the time, and there would be odd looks, and he would explain nothing, and then she, woman-like, must needs spoil the mystery by telling all about it, as if any one would not comprehend some jest in the matter! It was a home of rugs and books, and very restful. I liked to go there, where they both spoiled me, and where the softness and the perfume of it all made me useless and dissatisfied after I had come away. There is no reason in the average man. But in the Eden was one great serpent—not a real serpent, but a glittering one, like the toy snakes sold at Christmas time.

There is some weakness in our American training of girls. Visibly and certainly the woman who marries a man engages herself to conduct his household—to relieve him of all troubles there—because he is the bread-winner. But very few girls seem trained with such idea, though all girls look forward to a marriage and such mutually helpful compact between two human beings. It is, of course, the fault of a social growth, the fault of mothers, the fault of many conditions. And Jean did not know how to cook! She was a woman of keen intelligence, of all sweetness and all faithfulness, yet she found herself almost helpless when she became the chatelaine of the castle where Grant was to come to dinner.

It is needless to tell of all that happened. The woman was adroit in the engagement of domestics, and there were dinners certainly, and, possibly, good ones, but the knowingness of it all was wanting. He felt it, and wondered a little, but did not fret. He knew the woman. One evening they were together, after dinner again, just as they had been when he told her he would take her to the woods, and she lay coiled up upon a divan, while he sat beside her. It was their after-dinner way. She spoke up abruptly and very bravely:

"Grant, I'm a humbug."

"Certainly, dear; what of it?"

"I mean—and it's something serious—I really am, you know, and I want to tell you."

"Go ahead, midget."

She did not seem altogether reassured, but plunged in gallantly:

"You thought I would be a good wife to you. You thought I knew everything a woman should know who agreed to live together with the man she loved, and make the most of life. But, Grant, I was and am really a humbug! I don't know how to manage a house; I have to leave it to the servants, and I can see enough, at least, to know that it isn't what it should be. There are a thousand little fancies of yours I don't know how to gratify, and I want to do it so, Grant! What shall I do?"

He responded by saying that he was very fond of his little Dora Copperfield and that he would buy her a poodle dog. He added, though, that she mustn't die—he needed her!

There was a laugh in his eyes, and he was but the tyrant man enjoying the discomfort of the one being to him; but when she curled a little closer and looked up in earnestness, he relented.

"That is nothing, dear," he said, "save that I'm afraid you have a little work ahead. Yes, it is right that you should know what you do not. You must learn. It is nothing for a clever woman, such as the one I have gained. I look to you, love, for the home and all the sweetness of it, and I wouldn't do that if I did not think that in the end there would be all pride and comfort for you. Down East they call this or that woman 'house-proud.' I want you to be 'house-proud.' No wife who is that but is doing very much for all about her, and I won't say any more, except that you must let me help you."

And thenceforth ensued strange things. There were experiments, and there was even a cooking-school episode, Harlson, at this period, professing great weariness, and sometimes, after meals, simulating pains which required much attention, though drugs were vigorously refused. All he wanted was strictly personal care. It is to be feared that he was not honest as to details, though honest as a whole. And he would go marketing with the brown woman, who had become so practical, and they became critical together, and the gourmands, wise old men about town, whom he brought, occasionally, to dine with him, began to wonder how it was that they found such perfection at a private table. And, as for the woman, well, she passed so far beyond her clumsy Mentor that he became but as the babe which doesn't know, and had nothing to say in her august presence. He might talk about a cheese or a wine or some such trifle, but how small a portion of living are cheese and wine!

The first year of wedded life is experimental, though it be with the pair best mated since the world began. There is an unconscious dropping of all surface traits and all disguises, and a showing of heart and brain to the one other. Never lived the woman so self-contained and tactful that, at the end of a year, her husband, if he were a man of ordinary intelligence, did not know her for what she was worth; never the man so thoughtful and discreet that he was not estimated at his value by the one so near him. This I have been told by men and women who should know. I lack the trial which should give wisdom to myself, but I am inclined to accept the dictum of these others. It must be so, from force of circumstances.

It was pleasant to me to watch this man and woman. It seemed to me that the hard lines in Grant Harlson's face became, week by week and month by month, less harshly and clearly defined, while upon the face of his wife grew that new look of a content and ownership which marks the woman who sleeps in some man's arms, the one who owns her—the same look which Grant, with his broader experience and keener insight, used to recognize when he puzzled me so in telling whimsically, in the street cars, who were wedded, without looking at their rings. It may have been a fancy, but it seemed to me the two grew very much to look alike. It was in no feature, in nothing I can describe, but in something beyond words, in a certain way which cannot be defined. It may have been but the unconscious imitation by each of some trick of the other's speech, or manner, but it appeared a deeper thing. I cannot explain it.

They were not much apart, those two. Sometimes Harlson would be called away by some business or political emergency, and then would occur what impressed me as a silly thing, deeply as I cared, for each. He would get railroad tickets for two, and they would go riotously across the country, playing at keeping house in a state-room, and enjoying themselves beyond all reason. I explained often to each of them that it wasn't fair to the other; that he could attend to business better in some distant city without having to report to her at a hotel, and that it would be more comfortable for her in her own fair home; and the two idiots would but laugh at me.

The library was their fad together, for Jean was as much of a bibliomaniac, almost, as was her husband, and I confess I enjoyed myself amid the rich collection, made without precedent or reason, but, somehow, wonderfully attractive. They were whimsical, the pair, with books as with regard to other things, but the few who might invade their library were inclined to linger there. I always found a mingled odor there of cigar-smoke and of some perfume which Jean preferred, and I learned to like the combination. Maybe that was a perverted taste,—cigar-smoke and delicate perfumes are not consorted in the code of odor-lovers,—but, as I say, I learned to like it.

I have but little more to tell of this first wedded year of my dear friends. One incident I may relate. It occurred less than a year from the date of the outing in the woods. There were relations each of the two should meet, and he was very busy with many things, and it was, finally, after much thought, decided that Jean should go her way and he his for two long weeks; so they bade good-by to each other and left the city, in different directions, the same day.

It was just four days later when I got a note asking me to call at the house. It was from Jean, and she was a little shame-faced when she met me. Certain business complications had arisen in Grant's absence to which I might attend, and it was for this that she had summoned me; but she had an explanation to make. She did it, blushing.

"I went to my people, Alf," she said, "but it palled in a couple of days. That is all. I'd rather be here alone, where he has been, and await him here, than be anywhere else. It's foolish, of course, but you, who know us both so well, may possibly understand." And she blushed more than ever.

The next day there stalked into my office a man who asked me to lunch. It was Grant Harlson. There was a quizzical look on his face, and a rather happy one.

"I won't tell you anything, old man," he said. "I was only a few hours behind the girl. That's all. I suppose we might as well keep up the fool record we have begun. It suits me, anyhow."

And a single man, knowing nothing about such things, could give no opinion. I was abusive and sarcastic, but he insisted on buying a great luncheon.

CHAPTER XXVIII

THE APE

Given a man and a woman, married, loving each other, and
what a recent clever writer calls "the inevitable consequences"
ordinarily come and cause the inevitable anxiety, more,
doubtless, to the man than to the woman. There comes a time
when she he loves must bear him their first child. In primitive
existence this trouble to the man must have been much less,
must have been little more than the sympathy of an hour,
because, in nature, unaffected, there is seldom much of
suffering and almost never death prematurely. But we have
changed all this. We have violated gentle Nature's laws in our
ways of living, and inasmuch as we have done this, we have
lost, to such extent, her soft protecting hand. We breathe too
little of the pure air; we are lax in physical effort, and, even
though the individual man or woman be wise, he or she must
bear the burden of the errors of an ancestry or the evils of the
present. So, to the woman gentle-bred there comes a risk in the
undergoing of that which she has most hoped for since she
loved a man, and since she would be all there is of perfect
womanhood. There is peril, and she knows it, but is braver
than man at this time. There is peril, and he knows it, and he
is helpless and clinging as a child. What can he do? Nothing,
save to bring in a hard hour the presence of one who may not
bear a portion of the real trial. Yet this is something. It has
saved dear women's lives. There is something—we do not
quite understand about it yet—which is a band of more than
steel between two close together, and which holds back the one

sometimes from even the grip of that force seldom denied, which is named Death, the one who fills the graveyards.

And, one evening, there was a man in deep trouble, and in the morning he sat beside a bed in which was his small wife and beside her a tiny red thing, "rather underdone," he said, in the buoyant reaction which came upon him, for that was Harlson's way when he had emerged from trouble; and the small red thing was the son of the two of them. And who can tell what the man said to the woman. There are precious, sacred overflows of love, sweet outbursts of what makes life worth the living, never yet in words for all, never yet written in black upon some white surface. There is a sanctuary.

It was a healthy baby, and the mother was soon herself, and the most foolish of small women over it. I rather liked the young animal myself, for they let me see it when its days were few, and it clutched at my fingers in a way that won me. It was a curious young animal to me. It took to the water wonderfully, and all three of us together sometimes, when I would call, would summon the nurse and see the young villain bathe. This was when he was but a few months old. He was such a royal fellow, so brave and buoyant, that I fell in love with him. How could a lonely man help being foolish?

An odd name had the child. It all came from the hours, when, all danger passed, a proud and happy man sat upon a bedside and looked down into the face of a proud and happy woman, and, at times, studied the quality of the odd mite beside her, half hidden in the waves of pillow and of sheet. He would look at the thing's wonderful hands, and its wonderful pink feet, and have remarks to make. One hour he came in and examined the creature and repeated great words from some authority:

"How many people have ever taken notice of a baby's foot, except to admire its pinkiness and its prettiness?" said he. "And yet, to the anatomist, it is a revelation. Take, for example, the feet of a child of ten months, that has never walked nor stood alone. It has a power of grasping to some extent, and is used instinctively like a hand. The great toe has a certain independent working, like a thumb, and the wrinkles of the sole resemble those of the palm. These markings disappear when the pedal extremity has come to be employed for purposes of support.

"The hands and feet of a human being are strikingly like those of the chimpanzee in conformation, while the gorilla's resemblance to man in these respects is even more remarkable. The higher apes have been classified as 'quadrumana,' or 'four-handed,' because their hind feet are hand-shaped; but this designation is improperly applied, because the ape's posterior extremities are not really hands at all. They merely look like hands at the first glance, whereas, in fact, they are but feet adapted for climbing. The big toes cannot be 'opposed' to other toes, as thumbs are to the fingers, but simply act pincer-wise, for the purpose of grasping. Now, oddly enough, the 'infant's' feet have this same power of grasping, pincer-fashion, and the action is performed in precisely the same way. Advocates of evolutionary theories take this to signify that the human foot was originally utilized for climbing trees also, before the species was so highly developed as it is now. Also, they assert that the fact that the art of walking erect is learned by the child with such difficulty proves that the race has only acquired it recently.

"There, darling," he said, "you see how it is. We have but come into possession of a little ape! What shall we do?"

She was not troubled. In his eyes she saw that which is worth more to the young mother than all else the world can give, but she entered into the spirit of his mood. She replied, gently, that she didn't know what to do, but had he the bad taste to kiss an Ape? And he admitted that he had, and kissed the object gently, as if afraid of breaking it, and kissed the gentle mother a hundred to one.

I liked the Ape—for so they came to allude to that sturdy

babe. He may be my heir some day—though he was named, as Jean insisted, for his father—and I had many a frolic with him in his babyhood, when I was allowed to enter the sanctuary of that home. He was a little viking, a little raider, this child, conceived in the forest. There seemed to have come to him the daring and the vigor of outdoor things, and the force of nature. A great man-child was this.

I was not alone in the rejoicing over the infant, though really he was, it seems to me, as dear to me, the isolated man, as to his parents. They rioted in their vast possession, and were very foolish people. But why should I keep repeating that these two were very foolish people together?

They were like other fathers and mothers, in some respects, but one difference I noted. They seemed almost to adore the child, but he was never first with either of them. He but bound the two more closely together, and the looks of the man were sometimes almost worshipful as he looked upon the mother of his child. And she—she understood, and they were glad together. Their kingdom had been but enlarged.

It is not to be supposed that this whimsical couple—for they were really whimsical, these friends of mine, as must have appeared often in my account could rear a child without grotesqueries. The woman, I am afraid, was, before she became a mother, addicted to monkey tricks, even to the extent of bounding leopard-like upon the man from unexpected places, and the Ape was, in his early days, bred in a way barbaric. They had great times with the Ape.

One day Grant Harlson had his business for the day concluded early. He could reach home as a little after five o'clock, where dinner came at six. One of the fiercest of summer rains was falling. He started buoyantly. He wanted his wife and boy.

He reached the house and entered. No wife was there to greet him; no drunken-footed babe, for the Ape had learned to walk now, albeit unsteadily; not even a servant girl to make some explanation. He stalked through the house wonderingly, back to the kitchen, which looked out upon a green back-yard where they had erected a tent, and had there had dinners and inhaled the odor of the grass. He found in the kitchen the two girls, who were all delight, and exhibited but slight awe at his presence. He recognized that all was well, and looked out through the descending sheets of water.

There, beside the quaint tent set upon the green-sward, were two people. One was a graceful woman, one a sturdy, shouting child. Neither was garbed save in the simplest way. She wore a wrap of some sort, a careless thing, the boy a night-gown, and they were moving about in the warm rain and bathing in nature's way, and particularly happy.

The man was righteously indignant at all desertion of him. He shouted manfully, and at last attracted the attention of the pair. He told them to come in to him. As well have talked to the wild winds. He looked from the porch upon the riant, dissipated two, and commanded and cajoled and made tremendous threats, but to no purpose. He reproached his wife with unwifely disobedience, and with the crime of turning her own offspring against his father, and the two but mocked him! Then he disappeared, and appeared five minutes later in a frayed old swimming suit, and there was terror in the camp of the foe! He made a charge through sheets of rain, and a fair woman was, in most unmanly way, laid in a puddle, and her son set aloft in pride upon his prostrate and laughing mother. And high jinks ensued. So did these two conduct themselves!

But an hour later, when guests came to the dinner, the Ape had gone to his nursery without a whimper, and no more grave and courteous man or more stately and gracious dame sat down at table that evening in all the city of a million people.

CHAPTER XXIX

THE FIRST DISTRICT

The trouble with us in the First Congressional District was that we could not carry the Ninth Ward. But for this weak point we would have felt assured at any time. With the Ninth Ward eliminated we could control the district barely. With the Ninth Ward for us it would be a walk-over. But the ward belonged to Gunderson.

Gunderson employed three thousand men. He was not a party man, but he was a partisan; that is, he would get interested sometimes in a campaign, and when he did, each workman in his big manufactory must vote as indicated or go. And Gunderson did not like Harlson. The ways of the big employer were not what Harlson admired, and he had never tried much to conciliate him. So it came that in more than one legislative and local contest we had lost the Ninth Ward. And now Harlson was a candidate for Congress.

We were puzzled. "I'm afraid Jean will have to lock me out again," laughed Harlson, as we were discussing the problem one night after a committee meeting, and herein he referred to a funny episode, dating back to the time when the Ape was but a yearling. Jean, dignified, chatelaine, sweet wife and fond mother, was as interested in politics as in anything else that commanded her husband's attention at any time, and had learned from our conversations all about the Ninth Ward. We were confident one spring, and as Grant left home on the morning of election day he was informed that unless he came as a victor he must not expect admission to the home containing his wife and baby boy. He said he would return in triumph or upon his shield, but he did neither. At five o'clock in the afternoon we knew that we were whipped, whipped beautifully and thoroughly, and all because of that same black demon of a Ninth Ward, and the fact was so apparent that we became suddenly philosophical, and Grant turned to me and said:

"Come to dinner with me, Alf, and let's go now. What's the use of staying to the funeral? We'll eat a good dinner and smoke, and good digestion will wait on appetite, and we'll plan and say we'll do better next time."

So we left the hurly-burly and took the train, and were at Harlson's home a little before the dinner hour. Grant tried his latch-key, but it would not serve. He rang the bell, but there came no answer. Then there came a tapping and clatter from inside a window, and both of us left the porch to get down upon the sward and visit the window and investigate.

Inside the window, and smiling, was a small, brown woman, holding in her arms a crowing youngster, who was making a great ado and reaching out his hands toward his father. She raised the window just a little, and put a question, gravely:

"What is it that you wish, gentlemen?"

Grant intimated, humbly, that we wanted to get in and be given some dinner.

"Are you the gentlemen who were going to carry the Ninth Ward?"

"Yes."

"Did you carry it?"

"No."

The laughing face fell a little, but the stately air was recovered in a moment. "Well," she said, with dignity, "I'm very sorry. We do not wish to seem inhospitable, neither the baby nor I, but really we do not feel justified in harboring people incapable of carrying the Ninth Ward."

We explained and pleaded and apologized and promised, but for a long time to no avail. At last, after the dinner-bell had sounded, and after we had pledged ourselves to carry that ward yet or perish, we were admitted, only then, though, as was explained, for the child's sake. He was accustomed to climb upon his father after dinner.

So carrying the Ninth Ward became a synonym for any difficult feat with us, and if Grant accomplished this or that, or I made a good turn, or Jean gave her cook or dressmaker an inspiration, the Ninth Ward was referred to as having been carried. And here was that ward before us again in a greater emergency, and in its own proper person.

Gunderson had a wife. He would have owned two wives had the one in his possession been surveyed and subdivided properly, for she was big enough, abundantly, for two. She was the best illustration I ever saw of what difficulties burden the ignorant rich who have social ambitions. She was good-hearted, coarse, shy and hopeful. A woman may be coarse and yet timid, as I have noted many a time, and Mrs. Gunderson was of this type. She hungered for social status, but knew not how to attain it. To her burly husband's credit, he wished, above all things, to gratify his wife's ambition, but he was as ignorant as she regarding ways and means. He had learned that there was a limit even to the power of money.

Jean had met Mrs. Gunderson in a social way, but of course there could be no affinity between the two, and the heavy-weight matron, anxious for recognition, had hardly attracted a second thought from the small aristocrat. I do not know, by the way, that I have told of the social status of these friends of mine. I don't think either Grant or Jean ever gave the matter much attention. Grant was democratic in every principle, and yet, unknowingly, it seems to me, exclusive arbitrarily. He had those about him whom he liked, and they were necessarily somewhat of his kind. And Jean was, a little more thoughtfully, perhaps, of the same sort. Unconsciously they were the center of a set for admission to which rich men would have given money. But, as I said, this key is one of the few things money cannot buy.

The political fight was on, and fierce. We did good work in that campaign. The struggle was so keen, the supervision of everything so searching, that daring fraud became a thing impossible. It was simply a test of persuasion, of popularity and of relative skill in those devices which are but the moves upon the chessboard in a game where chances are nearly even. We were but moderately hopeful. Harlson was immeasurably the better candidate. He was, at least, earnest and honest, and would represent the district well. I asked once why he wanted to go to Congress.

"I'll have to think," he said, "to answer you in full. Firstly, I believe I want to go because I have some fool ideas about certain legislation which I think I can accomplish. I believe they'll like me better in this district, and, perhaps, in a broader way, after I have been there. Then I want Jean to enjoy with me all the mummery and absurdity of the most mixed social conditions on the face of the civilized globe, and, besides that, I've been invited to take black bass with her out of a certain stream in the Shenandoah Valley, and to kill a deer or two, with headquarters at an old house up in West Virginia."

He said this lightly, yet I knew it was not far from the full truth. He had ideas of changes and reforms, and was prepared to fight for them. As for Jean and the fishing and the shooting, that was a matter of course. He must get out to nature, and he must have her with him certainly. As for me, personally—well, we had fought the world together for many a year, and I never knew him to fail me, and I could not very well fail him. I worried about this battle, though we had gained steadily. There was an element in the district, led by shrewd politicians, of the graduated saloon-keeper type, which did not lack large numbers. Outside one ward, though we had practically beaten them, Grant had invoked everything. He had stood up squarely on every platform, and as well in every drinking-shop and den, and almost bagnio, and explained to whom he found the nature of the contest, and told them what he wanted to do, and what all the hearings were, and told them then to conduct themselves as they pleased—he had but put his case as it was.

And there are men among the thugs, and humanity is not altogether bad, even in the slums, and help had come to us from unexpected places. More than one man, brutal-looking, but with lines in his countenance showing that he had once been something better, came around and worked well, and all to his future advantage, for Harlson's memory of such things was as the memory of that cardinal—what was his name?— who never forgot a face or incident or figure. We were what the politicians call "on top," a week before election, save in that same Ninth Ward. I had seen old Gunderson myself. He was not what we call affable. I had to wander through many offices, and finally to send in my card. I found this burly man in his private room, looking over papers on his desk. He did not look up as I came in. I took a seat, unasked, and waited. It was five minutes before he turned his head. Then he muttered a "good-morning," for we had met before.

I tried to be companionable and easy. I returned his salutation, somewhat too effusively, it may be, and asked him about his business, and then wanted to know, in a general way, how be stood on the Congressional issue. He hardened in a moment.

"I don't know why I should support Harlson," he said.

"Isn't he honest?" I asked.

"Oh, yes, I suppose so," he grunted; "but he's not my kind."

"Is the other man?" I asked.

Even the burly animal before me flushed. The other man was but a tricky politician of the creeping sort, a caterer to all prejudices, and a flatterer and favorer. This everybody knew. But he had become a part of the machine, was shrewd, and, with the machine behind him, was a power.

"I've nothing to say about that; but Harlson's not my kind. He's like one of those stag-hounds. He has nothing to do with the other dogs."

"He's fought some of the other dogs," I suggested.

The man grunted, again: "He's not my kind." And I left the place. I had little hope of the Ninth Ward.

CHAPTER XXX

THE NINTH WARD

Unaccustomed to story-telling, it is possible that I have neglected chronology in this account. I referred just now to the time we couldn't get into Harlson's house because we hadn't carried the Ninth Ward and to the Ape crowing at the window in his mother's arms. Time passed after that, and, we all grew older, though, somehow, Jean did not seem to change, nor, for that matter, did Grant, though he was years her elder. But the Ape changed amazingly. He grew into a stalwart youth of fourteen, and became, about that time, addicted to a bad habit for which I reproved him in vain. He had discovered that he could pick up his little mother and carry her about in his arms, and he did so frequently. And his two younger brothers looked on enviously, and his pretty sister, the youngest of the group, with gravest apprehension. But Jean seemed rather to like it, though it was most undignified, and Grant, though he ruled his children well, seemed rather to approve of their treatment of her majesty. They were a happy lot together. The Ape was a good deal interested in the election, but was not allowed to talk outside the house. And Jean wore a serious look. She lived for one man.

I attended a party soon after my visit to Gunderson, and a very pretty affair it was. A very pretty incident I saw there, too.

What I saw was the advent of a big, blowsy woman, who was blazing with diamonds, whose face was good-natured, but who seemed ill at ease. She was like a Muscovy duck among game fowl. She was well received by the mass and overlooked by the few, and, being a woman, though of no acute comprehension, she understood vaguely her condition. She was unhappy, and there was a flush, upon her face.

I saw a small woman, neat in a gown of the Directory, it seemed to me, though of course not so pronounced, brought by apparent accident in contact with the big, blazing creature. The smaller woman was self-contained and of the blue-blooded in look and unconsciousness from head to heel. The two engaged in conversation, the one affable and interested, the other flushed and happy.

I do not know that I ever enjoyed a party more, yet I did nothing on that occasion, save to watch at a distance the two people I have mentioned. They drifted along together, and there was soon a group about them. Was not Mrs. Grant Harlson a social power, and was not a friend of hers fit friend and confidant for any one? I do not understand the ways of women. I do not comprehend their manner of doing things, but I know a thing when it is done. And when that party ended I knew that fat Mrs. Gunderson had risen to a higher plane than she had dared to covet for the time, and that she knew who had accomplished it. Grant was not present at the party, and of the incident I told him nothing then. I wanted him to note its possible sequence first.

The day of election came, and a great day it was. Outside the Ninth Ward we had passed beyond our hopes. That ward, though,—at least from the first reports, and we paid slight attention to the later ones,—remained, through Gunderson, sullen, incomprehensible, uncommitted. And at night, the voting over, newspapers began to show the bulletins as the ballots were counted and the returns came in. We were at campaign headquarters and got the figures early.

The scattering returns were satisfactory. Through most of the district they showed a gain for us over past encounters. The drift was all our way, but it was not big enough to offset all contingencies. There was nothing from the Ninth Ward yet. The counting was slow there.

It was eleven o'clock before the vote of any precinct from the Ninth Ward came in. It stood as follows:

Harlson, 71.

Sharkey, 53.

Harlson picked up the filled-out blank, glanced at it, and threw it down again.

"It's some mistake," he said; "that precinct is one of the stiffest the other way. Wait until we get more of them."

We waited, but not for long. The returns came fluttering in like pigeons now. The second read:

Harlson, 33.

Sharkey, 30.

There dawned a light upon me; but I said no word. I was interested in watching Harlson's face. He was a trifle pale, despite his usual self-control, and was noting the figures carefully. Added precincts repeated the same story. Harlson would take up a return, glance at it, compare it with another, and then examine a dozen of them together, for once in his life he was taken unawares, and was at sea. He left the table at length, lit a cigar, and came over to where I stood, leaning against the wall.

"What does it mean, Alf? If those figures don't lie, the Ninth Ward has swung as vigorously for us as it ever did against us. With an even vote in the ward the chances were about even. Now, unless I'm dreaming, we own the district."

"We do."

"But how is it? What does it all mean?"

"I suppose it means that Gunderson is with you."

"But how can that be?"

"Were you at Mrs. Gorson's party?"

"No."

"Jean was there, though."

"Yes."

"So was Mrs. Gunderson."

The man's face was a study worth the scrutiny. For a moment or two he uttered no word. The whole measurement of it was dawning on him. "The little rhinoceros-bird!" he said, softly.

The room was thronged, and there was a roar of cheers. The issue was decided beyond all question. The newspaper offices were flashing out the fact from illuminated windows. There were shouting crowds upon the streets. Hosts of people were grasping Harlson's hand. He had little to say save to thank them in a perfunctory manner. He was in a hurry to get home.

When I dined with Harlson the next day I hoped to learn some details, but I was disappointed. Jean was herself a trifle radiant, perhaps, for she remarked to me, apropos of nothing, and in the most casual way, that men were dull, and Harlson had little to say. Judging from his general demeanor, though, and the expression on his face, I would have given something to know what he said to his wife when he reached home the night before. Something no bachelor, I imagine, could comprehend.

And before the year ended Harlson had the Ninth Ward so that it couldn't bolt him under any ordinary circumstances.

CHAPTER XXXI

THEIR FOOLISH WAYS

It is, as I have said so often, but the simple story of two friends of mine I am trying to tell, but I wish I had more gift in that direction. I wish I could paint, just as an artist with brush and colors reproduces something, the home life in the house where much of my time was spent. I can but give a mechanical idea of what it was, but to me it was very pleasant.

A very shrewd politician Jean became, after the famous contest in which the Ninth Ward aided us to victory, and we were accustomed to consult her on the social bearings of many a struggle. In case she became too arbitrary on any occasion Grant had fallen into the way of calling the Ape, and asking him to remove her, whereupon the youth would carry off his small mother in his arms and insist that, as he put it, from a childhood expression, with a long "a," she "have herself." There was ever this quality of the whimsical about life in this home. And I am inclined to believe that the world is better for such a flavor.

The children, were well grown now, the family was rounded out, and Grant's mustache, gray when he was forty, was now grayer still, though Jean's brown hair showed yet no glint of silver. I asked one day after dinner, when we two were idling and smoking in the library, and Jean was hovering about, if she hadn't a gray hair yet, and Grant said no, without hesitation, though the lady herself seemed less assured. Then happened a curious thing, at least to me. I asked Grant how he knew so well, if even his wife, who, being a woman and fair to look upon, would be naturally apprehensive of any change in aspect, could not tell if a gray hair had come, and he but laughed at me. "Come here, Jean," he said.

She came and stood, beside him, close to me.

"Alf," said he, "I have a vast opinion of you, but there are some things I imagine you do not comprehend. You should have blended your life with that of some such creature as this, and you would have developed a new faculty. Now I close my eyes. Ask me anything about her—I don't mean about her dress, but about her head or hands, all you can see of the real woman."

I accepted the challenge, and there was great sport, and a little-great result. I made the inquest a most searching and minute affair. I asked him to tell me if there were any mark upon the neck, near one ear, and he described the precise locality and outline of a tiny brown fleck, no larger than a pin's head. He told of any little dimple, of any sweep of the downward growth of the brown hair, of any trifling scar from childhood. And of her chin and neck he told the very markings, in a way that was something wonderful. His eyes were closed, and his face was turned away from us, but this made no difference. He described to me even the character of the wonderful network in the palms of her little hands. Then he opened his eyes and turned to me, chaffingly:

"You see how ignorant is a man of your sort. Having no world worth speaking of, he knows nothing of geography."

I do not believe that even Jean herself knew, before, of how even the physical being of her had been impressed upon the heart and brain of this man. She listened curiously and wonderingly when, he was talking with his eyes closed, and when he opened them and began his nonsense with me she stood looking at him silently, then suddenly left the room. It was a way of Jean's to flee to her own room for a little season when something touched her, and I imagine this was one of the occasions. She had known for long years how two souls could become knitted and interwoven into one, but I do not believe that before this incident she had ever comprehended how her physical self, as well, had become an ever present picture upon the mind's retina of her lover and her husband.

I am worried, and bothered. I am a man past middle age. I shall never marry now, and shall but drift into a time of doing some little, I hope, toward making things easier for some other men and some women, and then—into a crematory. I have a fancy that my body, this machine of flesh and muscle in which I live, should not be boxed and buried in seeping earth to become a foul thing. That was an idea I learned from this firm friend of mine. I want it burned, and all of it, save the little urn full of white ashes which some one may care for, to go out and mingle with the pure air, and there to be one of earth's good things, and to be breathed in again and make part of the life of the maple leaf, or the young girl going to school in the morning, or the old-fashioned pinks in the front yard of the old-fashioned people, or the red roses in the florist's hot-houses. I have that fancy.

I am worried because I, clumsy, dull-thinking man, cannot tell what I wish to tell of a life I saw. I am worried because I cannot make others understand it as it was. It seems to me it would do some good in the world. It seems to me that many a man and woman, if they could know about Grant and Jean, who really lived,—for this is but a tale of fact,—would be now more loving and better men and women because of it. But I do not know how to tell of what I saw and what I knew.

Grant was over sixty years old at this time of which I write, and I am coming very near the end, and Jean was past forty, and the two were not much different from what they were when I first saw them together. I suppose it was partly because I had been with them so much that I did not note the changes nature wrought in this pair of her children, but certainly they were far younger than their years. They had found together the only fountain of eternal youth which exists or ever will exist upon this planet which threw off a barren moon and bred monsters and, later, mastodons and apes, and finally made a specialty of men and women. They laughed at time, and hoped for a future of souls after this trial. I saw it with my eyes, I heard it with my ears, when they spoke together. They were blended, and it made life worth the living. What I learned conveyed to me new things. It taught me that all there is in novels is not romance nor untrue. It taught me that a male and female of this species of ours may meet, and from the two may come an entity which is something very near divine. Why is it, I wonder, that the right man and the right woman out of the hundreds of millions meet so seldom at the fitting time, and that life is either so barren or so jagged and hurtful because of the non-meeting of those who should be mated? What a world this might be! Of course, though, there is some higher thought, and it is all right in some way.

They were what you would call religious, Grant and Jean. They liked the same church—it doesn't matter which it was— and attended regularly, and worshiped without much regard for its more narrow legends. They did not trouble themselves with the idea of the everlasting punishment of babes, nor the fate of the untutored heathen. They had, somehow, a simple idea that the human being who tried to do right according to his or her views was all right as to the future. They were not much in sympathy with what is called heretic-hunting. They had each read the story of the gentle Nazarene, and had failed to learn that there was more than one church—a church without either spectacular effects or creed bickerings. A church of the group who, at one time, clung to Him and His teachings, and so had shaped their course. To them a narrow, grim old Presbyterian—were he but honest and earnest according to his inherited brain and intelligence—might, some time, a year or ten million years from now, be walking arm and arm along the sidewalks of some glorious street of some New Jerusalem with the Jesuit of to-day, honest and earnest according to his brain and his intelligence. This is not reasoning. Was it a bad creed?

Stanley Waterloo

They were not afraid of old age as it came nearer, hour by hour and day by day, these friends of mine. They had pondered of it much, of course, for they were thoughtful people, and they had talked of it doubtless many times, for there was little of which they thought that the two did not reveal to each other in plain words; but they were not troubled over the outlook. They seemed to realize that the flower is no greater than what follows, that fruit is the sequel of all fragrance, and that to those who reason rightly there is no difference in the income of what is good in all the seasons of human being. I remember well an incident of one evening.

We had been playing billiards, Grant and I. He had a table in his house and had taught Jean how to play until she had become a terror, though the Ape had nearly caught up with her in skill, and there was, at this time, a great pretended struggle between them, and we had come up into the library after a hard after-dinner game. Jean came in, and we talked of various things, and looked at some old books, and, somehow—I forget the connection—began talking of old age. It was in the midst of our debate that Grant, after his insane way, suddenly leaped up and, standing beside me as I sat, proceeded to make me an oration. He talked of the friction of things and of the future of this soul or mind of ours, concerning the luck of which we know so little. And, while I may or may not have agreed with his general theories, I did not disagree with the one that the autumn is as much a part of what there is as is the spring, and that all trends toward a common end, which must be for the best in some way we do not comprehend, because we see, at least, enough to know that nature, wiser than we, makes no mistakes. "The fruitage 'goes'!" Grant exclaimed larkingly, and then, forgetting me for the moment, he caught up Jean, and, carrying her gravely about, repeated to her these lines:

> 'Grow old, along with me;
> The best is yet to be,
> The last of life, for which the first was made!"

And they were at least exponents of the belief they had, and it was to me an education and a comfort. I learned, what I could not profit by, that a man and woman together are more than twice one man or twice one woman, when the man and woman are the right two. It was like an astronomer studying the sun. And what warmth and light there was to look upon!

I have tried in these rambling words to tell how these two people faced the autumn and found it spring, since they were still together. I wonder why I made the attempt? It is but a simple relation of certain things which happened, yet I do not, somehow, get the pulse of it. It must be because I have known the people all too well. My heart is so much in what I try to say that I am not clear.

CHAPTER XXXII

THE LAW OF NATURE

Of what was the result of finally owning the Ninth Ward and the district I have only to say that it, of course, added to the reputation of one man—and of one woman as well, it may be added, for Jean in her necessary social functions grew in her way with Grant; but otherwise it made little difference. There was the family hegira to the capital, and much enjoyment of the limited attractions of the semi-Ethiopian and shabby but semi-magnificent city in a miasmatic valley, and it was, no doubt, some education for the children. To Grant it was a fray, of course, and to Jean it was enjoyment of his successes, and probably more sorrow than he felt at his failures. The successes were the more numerous. Jean herself never failed. She was an envied woman in the social world. She was a strong man's wife, and possessed of all tact and gentle wisdom in aiding him, but she was not a rival of the mere self-advertisers among the queens of a shifting society. She could not afford it, even had her inclination bent that way. She had absorbing riches. They were a man and her children.

When I brightened up, because my friends were coming back to me, was the great season of the year to me, as to them. When the family returned from the capital and reoccupied the home there was rejoicing. And what rioters we were! But once more, each time, it was said by Grant, and by me as well, the battle must be fought, and so came re-elections and the flittings. And, after all, it was good. It was not the rusting in the sheath.

And it came that there was another gallant fight on. The city Congressional district is not like the country one, where a man once firmly in the saddle may stay there for a quarter of a century. The city constituencies have the fault in make-up that their Congressmen are not selected as those who will do best for the districts, but because they have hands on the lever of some machine. Of course, there are always exceptions, as in Grant's case, but the rule prevails. And now there had been flung down the gauntlet of a clever adversary, and the battle was a warm one.

We both enjoyed this contest, for, though the struggle was likely to be sharp, we knew the issue was ours, from the beginning, and the whole thing, as Grant said, was like a hunting trip. But how it ended!

He had been out much at night, for it was a large district and there were many meetings, and had been as tireless as was usual with him. His thought was never given much to the care of himself, and in this campaign he appeared more than ordinarily reckless. Jean, watchful ever, reproached him and made him change his ways a little. Perhaps it was not all his fault that one day he felt ill. It was on the eve of the election.

We carried the day as we had hoped, and easily, and there was a demand for Harlson that night which could not be refused with grace. He was compelled to speak, and in the open air of a chill November evening. He told me he felt ill. When, late at night, we reached his home and he found Jean awaiting him, he turned to me and said:

"It's all right, Alf. I'll be myself again by morning. I'm where all that is good for me is, and should be well in no time. She will but pass her hands above my head, and—there you are!"

And we parted, as carelessly as usual, and as I went home I was speculating on what the revised returns would show the majority to be, not as to the outcome of Grant Harlson's indisposition.

Jean sent for me the next morning. I found a look upon her face which troubled me.

"Grant is not well," she said. "He came home late and spoke of an odd feeling. We cared for him, but this morning he was listless and did not want to dress and come to breakfast. He is in bed still. Please go up and see him, and then come down to the library and tell me what you think the matter is."

I went upstairs and found Grant lying in his bed and breathing heavily. I shook him by the shoulder.

"What's the matter, old man?"

He turned over with an effort, though laughing. "I don't know," he answered. "I only know I haven't been well since last night, and that there is a queer feeling about my throat and chest. I ought to be up, of course, but I'm listless and careless, somehow. By the way, what were the totals?"

I gave him the figures, and he smiled, and then with an "Excuse me, old man," turned his face to the wall. A moment later, as I sat watching him, alarmed, he roused himself and turned toward me again. "Won't you send Jean to me?" he asked.

I saw Jean, and she went upstairs, and when she came down her face was white. The Ape, rugged young man as he was, had tears in his eyes, and his brothers and sisters were crying quietly. I left the house, and an hour later a physician, one of the most famous on the continent, was by Grant Harlson's bedside. He was a personal friend of both of us. When he came down his face was grave.

"What is it, Doctor?"

"It's pneumonia, and a bad case."

"What can we do?"

"Nothing, but to care for him and aid him with all hopefulness and strength. He has vitality beyond one man in a thousand. He may throw off all the incubus of it. But it has come suddenly and is growing." Then he got mad in all his friendship, and blurted out: "Why didn't the great blundering brute send for me when first he felt something he couldn't meet nor understand?" And there were almost tears in his eyes.

The doctors have much to say about pneumonia. Doubtless they know of what they talk, but pneumonia comes nevertheless, and defeats the strong man and the doctors. The strong man it strangles. The doctors it laughs at.

All that medical science could command was brought to the bedside of Grant Harlson. The doctor, his friend, called in the wisest of associates in consultation, and as for care—there was Jean! He was cared for as the angels might care for a wandering soul. But the big man in the bed tossed and muttered, and looked at Jean appealingly, and grew worse. The strength seemed going from him at last—from him, the bulwark of us all.

All that science could do was done. All that care could do was done, but our giant weakened. The doctors talk of the croupous form of pneumonia, and of some other form—I do not know the difference—but I do know that this man had a great pain in his chest, and that his head ached, and that he had alternate arctic chills and flames of fever. His pulse was rapid, and he gasped as he breathed. Sometimes he would become delirious, then weaker in the sane intervals. He would send us from the room then, and call for Jean alone, and, when she emerged—well—God help me!—I never want to see that awful look of suspense and agony upon a human face again. It will stay with me until I follow the roadway leading to my friends.

The doctor gave the sick man opiates or stimulants, as the case might at any moment seem to need, and they had some slight effect; but there came a shallower breathing, and the quilts tossed under the heaving of the broad chest, fitfully. It reminded me in some strange way of the imitation sea scenes at the theater, where a great cloth of some sort is rocked and lifted to represent the waves. Only one lung was congested in the beginning, but, later, the thing extended to each, and the air-cells began filling, and the man suffered more and more. He fought against it fiercely.

"Grant," said the doctor, after the administration of some strong stimulant, "help us all you can. Cough! Force the air through those huge lungs of yours, and see if you can't tear away that tissue which is forming to throttle you!"

And Grant would summon all his strength, by no means yet exhausted, and exert his will, and cough, despite the fearful pain of it; but the human form held not the machinery to dislodge that growing web which was filling the lung-chambers and cutting off, hour by hour, the oxygen which makes pure blood and makes the being.

And the man who laughed at things grew weaker and weaker, and, though he laughed still and was his old self and made us happy for a brief interval, when he had not the fever and was clear-headed, and said that it was nothing and that he would throw it off, we knew that there was deadly peril. And one evening, when Grant was again delirious, the doctor came to me and said there was very little hope.

CHAPTER XXXIII

WHITEST ASHES

What is the mood of fate? Must strong men die illogically? What does it all mean, anyhow? About this I am but blind and reasonless. I wish I knew! The world is more than hollow to me, yet I have a hope, I'll say that. There was some one very like Jean, one whom I loved and who loved me, thirty years ago. Will she and I meet some day, I wonder? And what will she be to me then? I suppose I have the philosophy and endurance of the average man; but this is, with any doubt, a black world at times, and one in which there is no good. The breaking of heart-strings mars all music. I am alone and dull and wondering, and in a blind revolt. Why should all things change so, and what is this death which comes? There must be some future world. If there be not, what a failure is all the brutal material scheme.

One day Grant was clear of head, but weaker, and talked with me long of his affairs.

"I'm afraid I can't fight it out after all," he said, "though you mustn't let Jean and the children know that yet."

We talked more of what I should do if the worst came, and then he sent for the children. He addressed himself to the Ape first, the brave boy's eyes full of tears and his whole body trembling as he listened:

"My boy, you are hardly a man yet, but I know your manliness. If I cannot stay with you, you will become the practical head of the family. Make them all proud of you. And care for your mother always as you would for your own life or whatever is greatest." Then he called the others to him:

"You heard what I just said. I spoke to the Ape only because he is oldest. Remember that I have said this thing to all of you. I needn't say it, I know—my blessed boys and girls—you understand. But live for your little mother always."

I cannot describe what those young people said or did. It was most pitiful. It was brave and sweet, too. But they would not let their father die. He must not! They could not face the fact.

Jean came then, and we three were left alone for a time. She sat beside the bed, for he wanted his hand in hers when possible, and he spoke slowly:

"Jean, I don't know. There must be another world, as we have trusted. The great Power that fitted us to each other so will surely bring us together again. Let us look at it that way. We'll imagine that I'm only going to the country, and that you are to join me. That is all. I know it. God knows. He will adjust it somehow."

Jean did not answer. She but clasped his hand and looked into his face. I feared she would die of a bursting heart. From that time till the end she never left his bedside.

Murderous Death has certain kindnesses in his killings. Just before the end is peace. The struggles of this strong man became something fearful as the lungs congested, and the most powerful of anti-pyretics ceased to have effect, and then came the peace which follows nature's virtual surrender, the armistice of the moment. What trick of reversion to first impressions comes, and what causes it, none have yet explained, but long before the time of Falstaff men, dying, had babbled o' green fields. Grant Harlson, now, was surely dying.

The physicians had warned us all, and we were all about his bedside. As for me, thank God, the tears could come as they did to the children. But there were none upon the cheeks of Jean. Her sweet face was as if of stone; whiter than that of the man in the bed.

The convulsions had ceased, but his mind was wandering and his speech was rambling. It was easy to tell of what he was thinking. He was a little boy in the woodland home with his mother again, and was telling her delightedly of what he had seen and found, and of the yellow mandrake apples he had stored in a hollow log. She should help him eat them. And then the scene would shift, and he was older, and we were together in the fields. He called to me excitedly to take the dog to the other side of the brush-heap, for the woodchuck was slipping through that way! There was the old merry ring in his voice, and I knew where he was and how there came to him, in fancy, the sweet perfumes of the fields, and how his eyes, which were opened wide but saw us not, were blessed with all the greenness and the glory of the summer of long ago. Then his manner changed, and the word "Jean" came softly to his lips, and again I knew they were camping out together, and he was teaching to his wife the pleasant mysteries of the forest, and all woodcraft. There was love in his tones and in his features. The breast of the woman holding his hand heaved, and the pallor on her face grew more.

There was another struggle for breath, then a desperate one, and with its end came consciousness. Grant smiled and spoke faintly:

"It must he pretty near the end. I am very tired. Jean, darling, get closer to me. Kiss me."

She leaned over and kissed him passionately. He smiled again, then feebly took one of her little hands in each of his and lifted them to his face and kissed them; then held them down upon his eyes. There was a single heave of his great chest, and he was dead.

And the woman who fell to the floor was, apparently, as lifeless as the silent figure on the bed.

She was not dead. We carried her to her own room—hers and his, with the dressing-rooms attached—and she woke at last to a consciousness of her world bereft of one human being who had been to her nearly all there was. She was not as we had imagined she would be when she recovered. She was not hysterical, nor did she weep. She was singularly quiet. But that set, thoughtful look had never left her face. She seemed some other person. I talked to her of what was to be done. What a task that was, for I could scarcely utter words myself. She suddenly brightened when I spoke of the crematory and what Grant's wishes were.

"It must be as he wished," she said—"as he wished, in each small detail." Then she said no more, and all the rest was left to me.

She was quiet and grave at the funeral of her husband and my friend. She shed no tears; she uttered not a word. She listened quietly while I told her how I had arranged to carry out all his wishes about himself, or, rather, about his tenement. She did not accompany me. There came with me on that journey only the Ape, who was red of eye and vainly trying to conceal it all. How the youth was suffering!

I came to the home one day with an urn of bronze. There were only ashes in it, clean and white. Jean looked at them and asked me to go away. The urn was put, at her request, in her own apartments. It was sealed and stood upon a mantel of the room in which she slept. I do not believe she thought much of the ashes as representing the man who had gone away from her. She may have thought of them as precious, just as she did of a pair of gloves she had mended for him just before his illness, and which she kept always with her, but I believe that of the ashes, as of the gloves, she thought only of what her love had used in life and left behind. That was the total of it. It was the heart, the soul, the knowing of her that was gone.

How the Ape, how all the children cared for the small mother now! Never was woman more watched, and guarded and waited upon. She recognized it all, too, but said very little. Her soft hands would stroke the forehead of her first-born, or of her eldest daughter, or of any of the offspring of the two, the product of their love, and she would tell them that she was glad they were so good, but, gentle and thoughtful as she was, there was something lacking. She seemed in another world.

I talked to Jean. I tried to be a philosopher, to tell her of the children and of the broadness of life, and that she must drift into it again. She was kind and courteous as of old with me, but it was somehow not the same. And she grew weaker day by day, and would lie for hours, the children told me, in the room where Grant and she had been together all those years.

How can I tell of it! Jean, who had become my sister, who was part of Grant Harlson, drifted away before my eyes! It was harder, almost, for us than the fierce fight with death of the one who had been the mainstay of us all. Somehow, we knew she was going to leave us, and the grief of the children was something terrible. She listened to them and was kind to them, wildly affectionate at times, but she lapsed ever into the same strange apathy. We had the best physicians again. I talked with one of them. "What shall we do?" I asked.

He was a great man, a successful one, a man above the rut, and he answered simply:

"I cannot advise. The mind governs the body beyond us sometimes,—very often, I imagine. She does not want to live. That is all I can say. Drugs are not in the treatment of the case."

She grew thinner and thinner and more listless, and finally, one day, the Ape came to my office and said his mother had not left her room for a day or two. I went with him to the home which had been almost as my own.

I was admitted to Jean's room as a matter of course. I was one of the household. She was lying upon a great sofa, one Grant had liked. I asked her to tell me what to do.

She was calm and quiet as she answered. "There is nothing," she said. Then suddenly she seemed to be the Jean I had known one time. She raised herself up: "Alf, you were very close to us. Cannot you see?" She began another sentence, then stopped suddenly, and only smiled at me and said I was the nest friend ever two people had in all this world. She still spoke of two people. As if Grant were with us still!

How can one tell of the fading of a lily. No one ever told of it all. One day they sent for me, and when I came the sweetest woman lay upon her couch! She had talked with her children much that day, and told them many things—of plannings for their futures. She had, for the first time, told them of all their father had designed, or hoped, or guessed for each of them. And they had been very happy, and thought she would recover. And she had slept peacefully, and   had   not awakened.

I looked upon her face, and the smile upon it was something wonderful. It was one of the things which makes me believe there is some great story to it. There was none with her but her youngest daughter when she left us, and the child could not tell when worlds were touching. But upon that face was the expression which tells of what is all beyond. I do believe that, even before she quitted her earthly frame, dear Jean knew that she had found Grant again.

Why have I told this story of two people, which is no story at all, but only what I know of what has happened to those closest to me? There is no more of it. It ends with the deaths of them, and yet I do not know that it is sad. They lived and loved and died. They had more happiness than comes to one-half humanity. Their life was of the gold of what is the inner life of the better ones of this great new nation of a new continent. They lived and loved, and their children live, and will be good men and women.

*   *   *   *   *   *

I cannot understand the problem. No learning clears it. I only know that there were Grant and I, that there were bees and perfumes, and wild, boyish delights, and the older life, and the feverish life of a city, and the rare, great love I looked upon.

Choose from Thousands of 1stWorldLibrary Classics By

A. M. Barnard
Ada Leverson
Adolphus William Ward
Aesop
Agatha Christie
Alexander Aaronsohn
Alexander Kielland
Alexandre Dumas
Alfred Gatty
Alfred Ollivant
Alice Duer Miller
Alice Turner Curtis
Alice Dunbar
Allen Chapman
Alleyne Ireland
Ambrose Bierce
Amelia E. Barr
Amory H. Bradford
Andrew Lang
Andrew McFarland Davis
Andy Adams
Angela Brazil
Anna Alice Chapin
Anna Sewell
Annie Besant
Annie Hamilton Donnell
Annie Payson Call
Annie Roe Carr
Annonaymous
Anton Chekhov
Archibald Lee Fletcher
Arnold Bennett
Arthur C. Benson
Arthur Conan Doyle
Arthur M. Winfield
Arthur Ransome
Arthur Schnitzler
Arthur Train
Atticus
B.H. Baden-Powell
B. M. Bower
B. C. Chatterjee
Baroness Emmuska Orczy
Baroness Orczy
Basil King
Bayard Taylor
Ben Macomber
Bertha Muzzy Bower
Bjornstjerne Bjornson

Booth Tarkington
Boyd Cable
Bram Stoker
C. Collodi
C. E. Orr
C. M. Ingleby
Carolyn Wells
Catherine Parr Traill
Charles A. Eastman
Charles Amory Beach
Charles Dickens
Charles Dudley Warner
Charles Farrar Browne
Charles Ives
Charles Kingsley
Charles Klein
Charles Hanson Towne
Charles Lathrop Pack
Charles Romyn Dake
Charles Whibley
Charles Willing Beale
Charlotte M. Braeme
Charlotte M. Yonge
Charlotte Perkins Stetson
Clair W. Hayes
Clarence Day Jr.
Clarence E. Mulford
Clemence Housman
Confucius
Coningsby Dawson
Cornelis DeWitt Wilcox
Cyril Burleigh
D. H. Lawrence
Daniel Defoe
David Garnett
Dinah Craik
Don Carlos Janes
Donald Keyhoe
Dorothy Kilner
Dougan Clark
Douglas Fairbanks
E. Nesbit
E. P. Roe
E. Phillips Oppenheim
E. S. Brooks
Earl Barnes
Edgar Rice Burroughs
Edith Van Dyne
Edith Wharton

Edward Everett Hale
Edward J. O'Biren
Edward S. Ellis
Edwin L. Arnold
Eleanor Atkins
Eleanor Hallowell Abbott
Eliot Gregory
Elizabeth Gaskell
Elizabeth McCracken
Elizabeth Von Arnim
Ellem Key
Emerson Hough
Emilie F. Carlen
Emily Bronte
Emily Dickinson
Enid Bagnold
Enilor Macartney Lane
Erasmus W. Jones
Ernie Howard Pie
Ethel May Dell
Ethel Turner
Ethel Watts Mumford
Eugene Sue
Eugenie Foa
Eugene Wood
Eustace Hale Ball
Evelyn Everett-green
Everard Cotes
F. H. Cheley
F. J. Cross
F. Marion Crawford
Fannie E. Newberry
Federick Austin Ogg
Ferdinand Ossendowski
Fergus Hume
Florence A. Kilpatrick
Fremont B. Deering
Francis Bacon
Francis Darwin
Frances Hodgson Burnett
Frances Parkinson Keyes
Frank Gee Patchin
Frank Harris
Frank Jewett Mather
Frank L. Packard
Frank V. Webster
Frederic Stewart Isham
Frederick Trevor Hill
Frederick Winslow Taylor

Friedrich Kerst
Friedrich Nietzsche
Fyodor Dostoyevsky
G.A. Henty
G.K. Chesterton
Gabrielle E. Jackson
Garrett P. Serviss
Gaston Leroux
George A. Warren
George Ade
Geroge Bernard Shaw
George Cary Eggleston
George Durston
George Ebers
George Eliot
George Gissing
George MacDonald
George Meredith
George Orwell
George Sylvester Viereck
George Tucker
George W. Cable
George Wharton James
Gertrude Atherton
Gordon Casserly
Grace E. King
Grace Gallatin
Grace Greenwood
Grant Allen
Guillermo A. Sherwell
Gulielma Zollinger
Gustav Flaubert
H. A. Cody
H. B. Irving
H.C. Bailey
H. G. Wells
H. H. Munro
H. Irving Hancock
H. R. Naylor
H. Rider Haggard
H. W. C. Davis
Haldeman Julius
Hall Caine
Hamilton Wright Mabie
Hans Christian Andersen
Harold Avery
Harold McGrath
Harriet Beecher Stowe
Harry Castlemon
Harry Coghill
Harry Houidini

Hayden Carruth
Helent Hunt Jackson
Helen Nicolay
Hendrik Conscience
Hendy David Thoreau
Henri Barbusse
Henrik Ibsen
Henry Adams
Henry Ford
Henry Frost
Henry James
Henry Jones Ford
Henry Seton Merriman
Henry W Longfellow
Herbert A. Giles
Herbert Carter
Herbert N. Casson
Herman Hesse
Hildegard G. Frey
Homer
Honore De Balzac
Horace B. Day
Horace Walpole
Horatio Alger Jr.
Howard Pyle
Howard R. Garis
Hugh Lofting
Hugh Walpole
Humphry Ward
Ian Maclaren
Inez Haynes Gillmore
Irving Bacheller
Isabel Cecilia Williams
Isabel Hornibrook
Israel Abrahams
Ivan Turgenev
J.G.Austin
J. Henri Fabre
J. M. Barrie
J. M. Walsh
J. Macdonald Oxley
J. R. Miller
J. S. Fletcher
J. S. Knowles
J. Storer Clouston
J. W. Duffield
Jack London
Jacob Abbott
James Allen
James Andrews
James Baldwin

James Branch Cabell
James DeMille
James Joyce
James Lane Allen
James Lane Allen
James Oliver Curwood
James Oppenheim
James Otis
James R. Driscoll
Jane Abbott
Jane Austen
Jane L. Stewart
Janet Aldridge
Jens Peter Jacobsen
Jerome K. Jerome
Jessie Graham Flower
John Buchan
John Burroughs
John Cournos
John F. Kennedy
John Gay
John Glasworthy
John Habberton
John Joy Bell
John Kendrick Bangs
John Milton
John Philip Sousa
John Taintor Foote
Jonas Lauritz Idemil Lie
Jonathan Swift
Joseph A. Altsheler
Joseph Carey
Joseph Conrad
Joseph E. Badger Jr
Joseph Hergesheimer
Joseph Jacobs
Jules Vernes
Julian Hawthrone
Julie A Lippmann
Justin Huntly McCarthy
Kakuzo Okakura
Karle Wilson Baker
Kate Chopin
Kenneth Grahame
Kenneth McGaffey
Kate Langley Bosher
Kate Langley Bosher
Katherine Cecil Thurston
Katherine Stokes
L. A. Abbot
L. T. Meade

L. Frank Baum
Latta Griswold
Laura Dent Crane
Laura Lee Hope
Laurence Housman
Lawrence Beasley
Leo Tolstoy
Leonid Andreyev
Lewis Carroll
Lewis Sperry Chafer
Lilian Bell
Lloyd Osbourne
Louis Hughes
Louis Joseph Vance
Louis Tracy
Louisa May Alcott
Lucy Fitch Perkins
Lucy Maud Montgomery
Luther Benson
Lydia Miller Middleton
Lyndon Orr
M. Corvus
M. H. Adams
Margaret E. Sangster
Margret Howth
Margaret Vandercook
Margaret W. Hungerford
Margret Penrose
Maria Edgeworth
Maria Thompson Daviess
Mariano Azuela
Marion Polk Angellotti
Mark Overton
Mark Twain
Mary Austin
Mary Catherine Crowley
Mary Cole
Mary Hastings Bradley
Mary Roberts Rinehart
Mary Rowlandson
M. Wollstonecraft Shelley
Maud Lindsay
Max Beerbohm
Myra Kelly
Nathaniel Hawthrone
Nicolo Machiavelli
O. F. Walton
Oscar Wilde

Owen Johnson
P.G. Wodehouse
Paul and Mabel Thorne
Paul G. Tomlinson
Paul Severing
Percy Brebner
Percy Keese Fitzhugh
Peter B. Kyne
Plato
Quincy Allen
R. Derby Holmes
R. L. Stevenson
R. S. Ball
Rabindranath Tagore
Rahul Alvares
Ralph Bonehill
Ralph Henry Barbour
Ralph Victor
Ralph Waldo Emmerson
Rene Descartes
Ray Cummings
Rex Beach
Rex E. Beach
Richard Harding Davis
Richard Jefferies
Richard Le Gallienne
Robert Barr
Robert Frost
Robert Gordon Anderson
Robert L. Drake
Robert Lansing
Robert Lynd
Robert Michael Ballantyne
Robert W. Chambers
Rosa Nouchette Carey
Rudyard Kipling
Saint Augustine
Samuel B. Allison
Samuel Hopkins Adams
Sarah Bernhardt
Sarah C. Hallowell
Selma Lagerlof
Sherwood Anderson
Sigmund Freud
Standish O'Grady
Stanley Weyman
Stella Benson
Stella M. Francis

Stephen Crane
Stewart Edward White
Stijn Streuvels
Swami Abhedananda
Swami Parmananda
T. S. Ackland
T. S. Arthur
The Princess Der Ling
Thomas A. Janvier
Thomas A Kempis
Thomas Anderton
Thomas Bailey Aldrich
Thomas Bulfinch
Thomas De Quincey
Thomas Dixon
Thomas H. Huxley
Thomas Hardy
Thomas More
Thornton W. Burgess
U. S. Grant
Upton Sinclair
Valentine Williams
Various Authors
Vaughan Kester
Victor Appleton
Victor G. Durham
Victoria Cross
Virginia Woolf
Wadsworth Camp
Walter Camp
Walter Scott
Washington Irving
Wilbur Lawton
Wilkie Collins
Willa Cather
Willard F. Baker
William Dean Howells
William le Queux
W. Makepeace Thackeray
William W. Walter
William Shakespeare
Winston Churchill
Yei Theodora Ozaki
Yogi Ramacharaka
Young E. Allison
Zane Grey

www.ingramcontent.com/pod-product-compliance
Lightning Source LLC
Chambersburg PA
CBHW030316180626
46810CB00003B/1099